DANCING

IN

THE

RAIN

TANZANIA GLOVER

Cover Art by Aaronya Medici

www.tanzaniaglover.com

Booking With Love
332 S Michigan Ave

TANZANIA GLOVER

Suite #121- 2217
Chicago, IL 60604
www.bookingwithlove.com

To AJ,
This book would have been finished a lot sooner if it weren't for you, but if I could do it all over again I wouldn't change a thing. There are a lot of aunties out there who think they're the coolest, but we both know the title went to me the day you were born. I love you so much kid and I'll always be the Meg to your Chris.

1

DANCING QUEEN

Without a doubt men were naturally more violent and aggressive than women, but that didn't mean that I could completely let the fairer sex off the hook for bad behavior. Closely watching my mama and sister for the last twenty-six years had taught me that women were experts at hurting each other psychologically which usually left the type of damage that couldn't be seen.

My fans were the young and wild kind though and they didn't even try to hide their stingers when they felt slighted by me getting serious with somebody new. Like bees they surrounded, swarmed then stung her like she was an enemy covered in honey. And to think I had foolishly been calling them Theo's Angels for years when their actions as of late had proven to be more devilish than anything.

They blew up pictures of Tempest's feet and made fun of them for not being the cutest not knowing that she had practically been a ballerina since she could walk. They made up lies about other famous men she'd been with when we had both already laid everything on the table on our first date. But worst of all they body-shamed her for having a couple backrolls when I knew for a fact from meet and greets over the years that the majority of their asses weren't a size zero either.

To say I was surprised by the treatment would have been an understatement because most of them had embraced Nat during our entire on and off again relationship. She had been a part of my origin story though and ultimately they liked the idea of me sticking beside my high school sweetheart. But as for Tempest the message had been loud and clear—no new friends.

My natural instinct was to clap back and let them know there was nothing they could say that would ever make me want her any less. I considered the rolls a bonus feature not a glitch, her twisted toes were cute to me and I loved them in my mouth while I went deep, and I wouldn't have cared if she was a prostitute and hit every man that she ever knew. I would never give another man the chance to call her theirs again. And even though my manager Jonathan would have killed me for saying any of that online, I would've shouted it from the rooftops if Tempest had let me. But lucky for him being relationship goals was the last thing she wanted to do anyway. Instead she encouraged me to keep my fans happy and act single *within reason* while she spent up their little allowance money with my credit card that had been glued to her hand for months.

I was still new to having as many fans as I currently had so I didn't fight the discrete thing too hard, but I still went out of my way to show her the most attention on stage. And whenever she was brought up in an interview I made sure to deny our relationship but frame it as if I was still actively chasing her only she was out of my league which wasn't even a lie because she was.

And again it wasn't like we were going out of our way to be a secret since everybody on the tour knew the real situation anyway. We had done the professional thing during rehearsals, but the cat was officially out of the bag day one when she boarded my bus instead of the buses for the dancers and crew.

Obviously the bunk she had on my bus went unclaimed too so

all tour long we basically just used it for storage, extra luggage, and souvenirs from each city. That alone caused her to win everybody over because even though I finally had a bigger than average bus, space was still limited.

Even my younger sister and assistant DeeDee had eventually come around and embraced her like I knew she would despite them not getting off to the best start. I could tell Tempest was the type to hold a grudge too so I especially appreciated that she didn't just for me. She knew how much family meant to me so she played nice even though DeeDee and Nat were still friends too. Or at least they were for a while in the beginning.

Once the whispers of me and Tempest possibly being together became hollers, Nat started trashing me online. She claimed that she'd nursed me back to health after my car accident just for me to leave her for somebody else when I recovered. And even though it was a lie, from the outside looking in her spin seemed believable so Jonathan and my publicist Josie did what they did best and made it all go away.

I didn't even want to know how they'd done it or why she

had decided to go that route. I just wanted it to be over and thankfully it soon was. It left me feeling disappointed not just at who she had become but also for being yet another example of the person you started the relationship with not being the same person you ended it with.

I didn't let that keep me down for long though not that I could have anyway since The TheoSoul Tour had kept me occupied from the second the leaves started to change colors. It was my first time headlining an arena tour tand I'd chosen that name because Tempest always joked about my music being a genre in itself. Neo-soul vibes over trap beats. Pop lyrics looped on funk instrumentals. R&B harmonies stacked on alternative tracks. It was why despite having "the look" and the voice it had taken me so long to resonate with a wider audience. But everything fell into place when Tempest's viral dance video of my song kicked down the doors I'd been knocking on since I was sixteen.

Having her bless the tour with her choreography and energy though, that was the second best thing that had ever happened to me. Because with her they didn't just feel like repetitive but still disjointed shows anymore. They were full-fledged individual productions since no city got the same set. Switching things up each show meant we lived in rehearsals and it was a lot more work than I was used to, but it was worth it because it broke up the monotony that came with performing back to back.

It was obvious that just like me she had been waiting all her life for this moment and I finally saw firsthand why she didn't get to tour a lot—nobody wanted her to steal their damn show. Because even the quick dance breaks while I changed clothes had become highlights of the night thanks to the intricate storytelling she did with nostalgic music. She was a beast at finding good transition spots and interpolation was her forte so I even had her working with the creative director for the different set lists.

And as if all of that wasn't enough she knew the stage well too. She had incorporated all kinds of aerial shit that I never even had to think about before because of the smaller venues I'd been in.

Front, back, side or from above, every angle you see me I want to look good.

And boy did my baby look good up there. I knew from our first rehearsal that we would be using the stage as foreplay and seeing her in those leather leotards and costumes had me barely able to focus on stage sometimes. I would be wiped out after every show, but Tempest didn't get tired so I saved just enough energy to let her ride me to sleep most nights.

I was naturally pessimistic so I knew she had to have a con or two somewhere, but it had been six months and I still hadn't found something worth mentioning yet. And for the first time in a relationship I wasn't actively looking for anything either. I chose to just enjoy the never ending list of pros that came with having her in my world.

It felt good to be living out the lyrics to love songs again, just me, my girl and the road. And with just four shows left we were finally at the homestretch of what would now be the first leg of the tour since ten more dates had been added for the top of the year.

Usually by the end I would be tired and ready to get home to take an extended break, but I had more energy than ever and I attributed it to finally having both peace and a piece of home in Tempest with me all the time.

2
DANCING ON THE CEILING

Had to sweat her to get her
I ain't mind, she was worth that
Getting her back's another story
Ain't no takebacks

Newer fans that were late on the Theo Smith train had crowned me ToxicBae because of all the relatable but of course toxic relationship antics I'd written about on my debut album. Like everybody else I definitely had the potential for being on bullshit, but ultimately I was a lover not a game player. I was just a mood writer and that was what I had been experiencing with Nat and other girls around that time.

I was over the moon with Tempest now though so everything I wrote came out sounding happy as fuck and that was a problem for the label who wanted me to duplicate the success of the previous project. I was confident that the new love songs which were reminiscent of my mixtape days would take me to even bigger heights, but I knew my artistic integrity mattered none if it couldn't make them any money.

The compromise was fair though. I agreed to make the first single another toxic anthem that they could get behind and then we would sequence it so the album would reflect falling back in love again after losing it once. It seemed simple enough, but it had been weeks and the only decent lyrics I could come up with barely amounted to half of a verse.

Being on the road meant mostly missing Theo Thursdays online with fans, but I had been trying to show them some love before we made it to Oakland for a club appearance later that night. They liked getting to see me create songs from start to finish and sometimes even gave helpful lyric suggestions, but we were all stumped on where to go next for this one.

Had to sweat her to get her
I ain't mind--

"Theo, you know how much I love when you sing, right?" I heard Tempest say from behind as she came into my room on the bus without knocking. From her tone I knew she was getting ready to say something to contradict that so I was already smiling as I turned off the loud instrumental then ended the live video.

"Yeah so don't shoot the messenger, but everybody wants you to either come up with the next lines or give it a rest 'cause you're messing up our vibe," she said and I playfully kissed my teeth at her ganging up on me with them.

She was the only newcomer for the tour, but she fit right in by cheating at Uno and making up house rules with the rest of them. I on the other hand refused to play Monopoly, Spades, Dominoes and most of all Uno with black people because I had too much to lose. And I would be damned if my hypothetical cause of death could ever be traced back to somebody putting a *Reverse* on top of a *Draw Two* card.

"Ay Temp, real quick dump that nigga so he can finish the song!" my younger cousin Evan shouted down from the bunk area since my music was apparently keeping him from taking a nap. He had just joined us a few days ago after a show in Houston since he had finished his assignments long before the upcoming Thanksgiving break.

"I'm considering it," she said before asking him to come down and take her spot in the card game for a minute.

She was super competitive with DeeDee and my videographer about winning so if she had suddenly planned on sitting out a round I knew there had to be something else besides my music on her mind. I sat my guitar down and watched as she closed the door behind her then joined me in bed. She laid her head in my extended arm like she always did, but the way she looked up at my face told me we needed to talk.

"That's enough," she began, letting the two words slip out of her mouth like the breath that had just come before it only they had obviously been inside of her for a while longer.

"What are you talking about?" I asked knowing exactly what she was talking about but that she wouldn't go into full detail while we were still on the bus because everybody heard everything even if they didn't want to.

As expected she just held up her hand and the thin platinum cuffs that she wore gently banged against one another. Unsurprisingly the diamonds in the chain that they'd been made from had been fake, but I got the setting melted into bracelets as kind of a keepsake or a reminder for her. She was safe now.

"I already told you that ain't got shit to do with me," I said dismissively before reaching over for my phone, but her grabbing onto my face forced me to give her my undivided attention.

"Then how do I have EJ's chain on my wrist?" she asked just above a whisper even though she had already heard my lame excuse of just buying it from some guys when she first recognized it. "And why has he coincidentally had *so much* bad luck since I told you what he did to me?"

She had probably been referring to him getting jumped again recently because he had already been caught slipping a couple times over the summer. Or maybe she was talking about his house getting raided and all the years he was facing from the gun and drug charges. Or it could've been any number of things that'd happened to him that he didn't make public since I had made it my full-time job to torture that nigga until I felt satisfied.

See learning more about her past had been both a gift and a curse for me. Her opening up and giving me the gritty details of what she'd been through let me know she trusted me with her secrets, but it broke my heart too knowing that I wasn't around to protect her somehow even retroactively.

It had been different when I knew the cause of her miscarriage was a nameless man from her past that didn't know how to keep his hands to himself. But when she didn't want to go to a friend of a friend's album listening party with me because **he** might be there, I knew I had to do something. So I did it.

I was far from a street dude and I didn't rap or rep any sets like he did. In fact I had never even thought to do anything to jeopardize tmy freedom before, but at the same time I didn't play about mine and I didn't want her feeling scared ever. So I decided to show her better than I could tell her that she didn't have to be by proving that he wasn't invincible.

I reasoned that I was at least smart about it and didn't personally do anything even though I'd wanted to because my hands worked just fine. But I was positive by now that he had gotten the message all the same since everybody in LA knew somebody. But with all the trouble he had found himself in recently though I guess he knew better than to retaliate then become the latest example of a rapper getting bodied by a singing nigga.

"Karma," I finally answered after she had repeated her question to me. "You can only hurt people for so long without eventually getting what's coming to you."

"You're right, but I promise you that me not being in his life is all the punishment he needs," she assured me then punctuated her assertion with a sweet kiss on my lips. I still winced at the sudden intruding thought of her not being in my life anymore because of how much it would fuck me up.

As I listened to her explain that her worrying wasn't out of concern for his well-being but mine, I decided to let her have her way. My baby truly had a heart of gold and it definitely didn't hurt that the perfect set of titties was sitting on top of it either.

"Alright. If you say it's enough then it's enough," I gave in before returning her kiss to sender and letting a hand grab onto the aforementioned tig ol' bitties. "You locked the door?" I asked her after checking the time to see that we were still a few hours out from Oakland.

"No and we'll be at the hotel in no time so just hold tight," she said predictably even though she had been fucking up the bed for the whole tour whenever she was in the mood.

I knew her horny ass wouldn't be able to stick to her *No Sex On The Bus* rule back when she first brought it to me, but we had both agreed on abstaining on show days after I was visibly tired on stage a couple times.

"C'mon. The show's not even until tomorrow."

"Yeah but you have to be in that club late tonight and we don't need you falling asleep like you did last time," she reminded me as I continued to play with her nipples then sucked a sensitive spot on her neck.

"Mm Theo stoooop! Jonathan is right there and I am not getting in trouble for you. He just started liking me a little bit," she laughed out as she tried to slip out of my arms, but I caught then threw her right back on the bed before she could get far.

I almost got mesmerized by the way her breasts jiggled as I pinned her down because they had a hypnotizing, natural bounce. She kept them secured during rehearsals and performances, but I loved getting to see them out and free on the bus.

"Nah J loves you. Everybody loves you."

"Yeah everybody except your mama because that woman cannot stand me," she said definitively which instantly made me scrunch up my nose and loosen my hold as I forgot about my mission for a second.

"Where did that come from? My mama loves you."

"No. She's tolerating me with a smile because she knows *you* love me and I have you wrapped around my finger," she said smugly just to tease me, but it still made me pause to think about what she meant as I laid down again.

She hadn't misspoken about my feelings for her, but I still hadn't directly used *that* word when talking to or about her to anybody. Although I really meant it when I said it to fans, I used it so much the past few years that it had almost lost meaning so I preferred showing her instead.

"Nah you're wrong. I swear she really fucks with you. And you're talking big shit for somebody that's about to be biting the pillow in a minute."

"Not if I pull out those moves I learned from her ladies' night party. I'll finally show and not just tell you how she's kept your daddy at home all these years," she joked knowing full well that I'd been trying to get the details of that party out of my head for months now.

"Look I told you all of that

was cap. My mama is a saint and me and DeeDee are adopted."

"Yeah adopted, but you specifically are sitting up here looking just like her."

"Alright that's enough about Mrs. Smith because I'm about to segway into asking you to at least let me eat it for a little while," I begged like I was a dog in need of a treat.

By now she was hip to me using head as a ploy to get her legs open because I knew it always made her crave my dick afterwards. But it wasn't like it was some daunting chore for me anyway and sometimes I wondered which one of us enjoyed it more. I forgot all about singing when my head was between her legs because feeling her pussy trembling on my tongue had become my favorite pastime.

"How many times do you think I'm gonna fall for this?" she asked sarcastically but still piped down and stopped resisting when I put my hands in her shorts and landed on her clit.

"You're gonna fall for it every time. Now take these off," I demanded feeling triumphant until she told me to go brush my teeth first because she could taste the garlic from the leftover wings I'd just had for lunch.

"Ay you tryna say my breath stinks or something?" I asked as I blew into my hands to get a whiff. She laughed so hard at my reaction to it that even I had to let out a chuckle at the silly mood she was obviously in.

"No! You know you always smell good, baby. That's why I noticed it was lowkey humming now," she teased as I jumped up to go to my private bathroom on the bus. "And wash your hands while you're in there too. You were just touching that dirty little guitar," she added since I tried to collect every vintage one I came across.

"I already know. Janet taught me the importance of keeping my nails clean all the way back in *Poetic Justice.*"

"Okay that's enough about Ms. Jackson too. I swear you haven't stopped talking about that woman since she announced that damn tour and I'm really starting to rethink taking you."

"Aw don't be like that. Why would I want Ms. Jackson *if you're nasty* when Ms. Randall *even if you're not* is already right here getting naked in my bed?" I asked as I prepared to trade my mouth full of toothpaste for a mouth full of Tempest.

I knew Evan was probably somewhere punching the air when I put the music back on because by now everybody knew what it meant and that it would be on for a while. It was intended to drown us out some, but it never actually worked because the goal was to always make Tempest hit notes that even I couldn't.

She knew that too which was why she tried being extra quiet, but I took that personally. My nondisclosure agreements had been passed around like candy before anybody even got their contracts so I didn't particularly care who heard what.

This is my bus. Make them niggas uncomfortable.

I never would have imagined

that trying to turn her out could have a boomerang effect on me, but it had and I did everything imaginable to get her off because nothing was off limits anymore. I'd thought that my tongue had been around the world and back before her, but it had been stamped so much recently that it needed a new passport. And teaching my baby cougar a few new tricks definitely had us both purring every time.

When I came out of the bathroom Tempest was bare from the waist down, but that wasn't bare enough for me and I let her know that while I led by example and changed into my birthday suit. Hearing, touching, smelling and of course tasting her were all important parts of my sensorial stimulation, but I was always a visual kind of learner so I needed to see everything too.

There was plenty of natural sunlight to go around and the LEDs were LED-ing, allowing me to get an eyeful of the soft curves, hard nipples and open legs that were calling out to me. But there was still something else missing to kick shit up a notch.

The mirror.

I cleared away the pile of clothes that was blocking the full length I'd had strategically placed on her side of the bed. I had the same exact set up at home since I really liked watching her face when I first pushed in from the side. Because even though she knew it was coming, she still always seemed so surprised at how much I filled her up. Like she forgot how big I was but loved the not so gentle reminder all the same.

She had already been peering down at me as I got situated on my knees so I saw the exact moment she felt the residual cool mint from my tongue hit her sensitive bud. Her eyes and hips bucked at the same time letting me know that it was a *Wild* card she wasn't expecting to find outside of the latest round of Uno.

Thankfully my locs were freshly retwisted which meant her fingers couldn't get tangled in them how they had when we were in the same position a couple days prior. Some things stayed the same though, I noted as I immediately went to work getting her dripping wet so that I could play around in her puddles soon.

Even lying flat on her back with her legs wide and her love on display, Tempest never could stop dancing. Her limited movement only allowed her to slowly wine against my mouth though as it collected the most refreshing drops of water. Try as I might I never could have just one sip so I quenched my thirst every chance I got and made time for it even when I didn't have any.

It was a cliché, but she really had become something like an addiction and sometimes I felt like I was getting a fix when I consumed her. She even had me wondering if there really was something to soul ties, voodoo, the divine feminine, I don't know, something. Because something just felt right about pleasing her in that specific way and for the umpteenth time I left her shaking, cursing and in need of a *Slippery When Wet* sign.

Before sinking everything I had on me into her, I had teased her clit with the tip for as long as I could stand it, but after a minute of that I swore her slick, molten grip practically pulled me in on its own. Logically I knew it was just pussy and it functioned the same as any of the others I'd been in before.

But there was just something about Tempest's that had me convinced I was experiencing a piece of heaven every time I was inside of her. It really did have to be something godly about it though because there was just no other explanation for why I felt compelled to tithe her fine ass so much.

An errant bump in the road suddenly sent me flying deeper than I'd intended to go and with the exhibitionist in me already feeling like we were semi-fucking in public, I had no control over how quickly my nut had come.

"Fuck Temp. My bad. Where you want it?" I grunted in her ear but didn't get a verbal response. Instead she answered by squeezing me with her legs and pulling me in closer.

And it didn't matter how many times she had done that before, every single time it made my ending even happier. Making babies wasn't on the agenda just yet and it probably wouldn't be for a while for a bunch of reasons, but the mind games I played pretending like this time might be the time had me sputtering and making sure she got every swimmer.

It took a while for my breathing to return to normal, but she laid there as patient as could be while I got myself together since my weakened arms couldn't hold me up anymore. Eventually we laughed about me setting a new quickie world record, but I was grateful that she knew how good her shit was and never tripped when she got the best of me off rip sometimes. Because even after fighting for my life in round one she knew I would always come back harder than Hoodie Melo so she could get hers again too.

"Theo, you're so nasty. Why are you always looking after?" she whined as she tried to clamp her legs shut, but I held them open to examine the fine details of my latest masterpiece.

"What, an artist can't admire his own work now?"

After peeing and cleaning herself up in the bathroom she settled back into my arms with her head on my chest and a leg thrown across me. Her sweet smelling hair tickling my nose finally made me remember to tell her that she had been right about her new brand of dandruff shampoo soothing my dry scalp.

"Told you it would help. Remind me to order you some when we get home, okay?"

"When did we get a home together?" I asked sarcastically before she lifted her head just to see mine as she mushed it.

"You know what I meant. Nobody wants to live in your gross little bachelor pad anyway," she said sounding salty and I thought it was cute because it wasn't like it was a bad idea since I made her stay over so much anyway.

I'd never shared a room let alone an apartment with anybody before, but I figured if we had managed not to kill each other for the two months we'd been out on the road then officially sharing my place would probably be a breeze in comparison.

"Okay where you want to live then?" I asked seriously, but she shrugged because she probably hadn't put any thought into it before now. "Well when you figure it out let me know."

She nodded since she didn't have anything else to say on the subject, but she still couldn't resist pulling on my nostrils to tease me about what she had been saying from the start.

"Wide open, choirboy. At this point I can almost see what you're thinking."

For a while she played around with the neatly cut hair on my face that was still coated in her love, but by the time her hand found itself below my waist she obviously wasn't in the mood for games anymore. Slow strokes from base to tip had me pointing to the sky again in no time so when she sat up I assumed she was getting ready to *Hop On Pop*. Instead she decided to inch down and put her lips in my lap.

Her stare game during head was a killer on its own. I didn't ever recall one instance of her blinking as she dragged her wet lips up and down on me, but then again it wasn't exactly like I could keep mine open long enough to keep score. I wanted to let her finish me off again, but after bussin' for a second time I would need to recharge for a lot longer so I told her to ease up so that we could focus on her again first.

She pouted when I pulled myself from her mouth, but there was a full-on frown when the phone that I'd forgotten to silence announced who was calling and interrupting us.

It was Maya also known as the other half of the most

unbelievably fake relationship known to man. Jonathan managed her too and he'd concocted the whole thing over the summer to promote our duet from her album, but literally nobody believed it for a second.

Despite dating men sometimes everybody knew Maya was more into girls and the rumors about me and Tempest were heating up back then so it ended up being a total waste of time. But even still Jonathan wouldn't admit defeat and had us ending the show with the song every night and acting flirty under pictures every now and then.

Of course Tempest didn't seem affected by any of it until they finally met on the set of the video and Maya couldn't stop joking but not really joking about us possibly having a threesome. That wasn't my thing anyway so I just laughed it off and told her I was stingy with my girl, but I would've been lying if I said I wasn't a little tempted at the thought.

Tempest must've been able to see what I was thinking back then too because the second we were alone again she dropped her phony smile.

"Don't even think about it. If just me and you ain't spicy enough

then I don't know what to tell you. Better put a ghost pepper up your ass or something."

As far as putting on a good show though, Maya had been a cool addition to the tour and the fans went crazy for her too. But still I knew to keep my distance and keep it professional because even besides the Tempest thing, her bus was a lot rowdier than mine. I didn't judge because it was harder for some people to get on stage night after night and even we had a little weed and alcohol for whoever wanted to indulge and relax. But they had the real party favors over there and out in the open too.

It didn't matter how long I had been in the industry I would never be prepared for people to just start casually doing coke let alone offering me some like it was a stick of gum. They made me feel like a choirboy for real because I dared to be different and only drank in moderation to protect my voice. Again I had fun too, but I took my craft too seriously to ever get into that kind of thing.

After reaching over to turn my phone off I just knew that me and Tempest were about to get right back down to business, but instead she sat up and asked me if I'd noticed Maya getting a little too into the fake thing with me on stage lately.

"Well J did say she wants to start acting. Maybe she's just really getting into the role," I joked before trying to bypass the topic with a kiss only it was a lost cause since she had a follow up in mind.

"Are you attracted to her?" It was obviously a trick question, but I didn't want to lie to her over something as dumb as that since anybody could see that the girl was far from ugly.

"She's a'ight. Teeth are a little big though," I said throwing in the only visible flaw I could think of. "But you, you got good teeth."

"So you're saying I should

cancel that consult for veneers? I really want that XXL, all caps mouth look that everybody's wearing these days," she said sarcastically.

"Definitely cancel that shit. You're perfect already and I have a hard enough time fitting my dick in there anyway."

"Theo, when has anybody ever struggled to fit your dick anywhere?"

"You really think my shit is little?" I asked already knowing she was messing with me. "Tough crowd. Give a woman eight long inches and watch her still complain."

"Seven."

"Eight."

"Seven," she said standing as firm as I was again after she reached down and took hold of me.

"Either way you still can't take it all. But for real you don't have to worry about Janet, Maya or anybody else, Temp. You know we're in this for life, right?"

"I know. They're them, but I'm **me** and you wouldn't risk losing this because you won't be able to find me in somebody else."

Her tone wasn't threatening at all. Just facts and what I had known from the very beginning. Still hearing it from her instantly made me rock up. Just the sight of her was enough to get me stiff, but that confidence and air about her that said she knew she was one of one would always be undefeated.

"Yeah I know. Now turn around and let me get **you** one more time from the side."

Without protesting she rolled over and poked it out just how I liked since she knew better than anybody what those solid *eight* inches could do from that position.

3
DANCING IN THE DARK

had been performing in clubs long before I was even allowed to legally drink so for me they had lost their luster a long time ago. But going to a club with somebody like Tempest was an experience that everybody should have at least once in their life.

Most of the time when everybody went out she would hang back at the hotel for alone time or to catch up on sleep since she was more introverted than I had realized early on. I'd assumed she had a bigger than life personality and active social life because of her stage persona and while she had her moments she seemed to like her solitude more.

Meanwhile I'd always been the fidgety type that had to keep busy all the time so being with her had brought out a calm side I didn't even know I had. She taught me that I didn't always have to be creating or plotting. We could just lay together sometimes. Sleep. Chill. Be. And it was enough.

Whenever she did decide to pop out though she was always

with the shits and easily the life of any event she stepped into. While other people were posted up and rapping lyrics into their phones, she was actually out there dancing and fucking shit up. Watching her hit marks perfectly and performing extensive choreography on stage almost every night never got old, but seeing her body rocking and swaying to beats for the sheer enjoyment of it was just something different.

She was in tune with her body and what it could do like I'd never seen before and her fluid movements drew crowds without trying. She called it well-developed bodily-kinesthetic intelligence since she knew all the technical terms, but I just called it *it*.

And I would never say it aloud, but I almost considered her classes to be a rip-off sometimes since they gave people false hope that they too could be as good as she was with enough practice. In reality she could only teach them the steps though because the natural rhythm and magnetism couldn't be bought with a billion.

She decided to take a break from entrancing everybody around her to come find me when the beat dropped to a song I'd helped produce at least a year or two ago. The rapper who it belonged to had only just decided to release it this past summer though and I'd completely forgotten about it until Jonathan said he wanted my vocals for a new hook. With Tempest solidly on the brain at that point it was no surprise what I came up with.

Bad Amazon in my bed
And I ain't even in my Prime era
Good girl, even greater head
Always deliver on time with her

For a minute she acted like it was just us in the function as she wrapped her arms around my neck then rapped the few bars she knew I'd ghostwritten about her. She was definitely past the point of being tipsy because I knew she thought the Amazon thing was corny and hated that I'd mentioned how amazing the head on her shoulders was.

Usually she held her liquor like a champ and could drink anybody under the table, but every now and then she got touchy feely and couldn't keep her hands off of me. It would have been easy to just blame it on the alcohol like before, but the more likely culprit was Maya and company being present since she was being paid to be there too.

I would flat out deny it if she

ever accused me of it, but a part of me liked knowing that she still got jealous too. I didn't want to be with anybody else or between anybody else's thighs and I didn't see that changing anytime soon, but yeah she had me so strung out that sometimes I needed the reminder that she wanted me just as bad.

I looked up and caught Jonathan's eye who was signaling for me to maybe stop the PDA with my real girlfriend since we were in a club full of people including the fake girlfriend that for some odd reason nobody believed I was actually with. I knew he was right so I quickly kissed the top of Tempest's head then sent her back into the wild to continue doing her own thing while I did mine.

By the time everybody was ready to go they had to turn the lights on and cut the music to get her cute drunk ass to stop hitting the Dougie. It was way past midnight and technically a show day, but from the way she looked at me with her now low and slanted eyes I sensed sleep wasn't on the schedule. Obviously I didn't care about bending the rules either since I already had my hand up her dress in the back of the sprinter, but I stopped teasing her when she made

DeeDee and the other girls promise not to let Maya near me when she was gone.

Thinking that she was joking I asked her where the hell she thought she was going, but it was like she instantly sobered up when she realized what she had said. They all laughed at us, figuring that she was just drunk and rambling, but it was clear she had slipped up by how quiet she got for the rest of the ride back to the hotel. I didn't even have to press her for details when we got in either because she was suddenly in the mood to talk.

"Remember when I met up with my friends from school in

New York?" I nodded since I definitely couldn't have forgotten how she'd disappeared until almost showtime then with her Alvin Ailey American Dance Theater crew. I'd wanted to tag along to meet everybody, but she claimed to not want to be the girl who brought her man along to a girl's day.

"Okay so we didn't really do brunch and a movie. It was actually kinda like a rehearsal audition thing for Bianca King's Abu Dhabi concert to see how I fit with everybody and she loved me."

She fired her words off a mile per minute before plopping on the bed, but when I managed to Ash Ketchum all I could do was smile. Bianca King was music industry royalty and working with a legend like her in any capacity was an automatic career boost. It was why despite just getting my feet wet in arenas, I'd already had Jonathan working on securing a spot to open for her summer stadium tour even though we knew it was a reach.

"Wait that's dope! She wants you to do some of the choreography with Ainsley?" I asked about her old friend who was the dance captain.

"I don't know yet. I would just be a dancer for now, but it's okay. I can just show up and not have to think so much. And baby, I just know if I do a good job with this then I'm practically a shoo-in for her Revival tour next summer."

For a minute there it might've looked like I was more excited than she was as I hugged and congratulated her on everything, but then it suddenly dawned on me why she had been sitting on the good news for the past couple weeks. Jonathan had joked before that she'd stalled on signing the tour extension contract to get more money since he had lowballed her big time, but I'd already planned on giving it to her from my own pockets because even though it was still back there, she had definitely worked hard enough to work all of that ass off.

For the first time I suddenly felt my genuine joy for her wavering. On one hand I knew it was a once in a lifetime opportunity that nobody deserved more than her, but I couldn't help but hate the timing of it all since it would interfere with us personally and professionally in the present and potentially going forward.

She was still beaming and going on and on about everything she had been keeping from me so

I tried hard to not let those thoughts show on my face. I had never been able to convincingly hide how I felt though so she picked up on it immediately.

"Nothing's wrong. It's just…you really didn't have to lie to me about this, Temp."

"I know and I'm sorry, but I was flabber *and* gasted at the entire situation," she joked trying to make light of it, "and I didn't want to jinx it. I haven't even told my mama yet."

"Right, but you haven't been with her every day like with me so it's different. And you're not leaving your mama's tour to go rehearse for a single concert for somebody else.”

"Yeah, but it's not like y'all really need me here anymore. The show will go on," she said dismissively and I could hear her frustration level getting ready to pull up next to mine.

"I need you. And you're just already planning on dipping on touring with me next summer?" I asked since Jonathan had technically already gotten me on a mostly rap tour, but I'd been holding out since my sets were for grown women not white kids and niggas stinking up the venue with Kush.

"Well I don't know yet. If it clashes then I'll just catch your next one," she said like it was that simple and it actually must have been since she didn't even have to think about putting me in second place.

"Just like that you're picking her over me? I must not be putting it on you like I think I am. Shit maybe it is only seven inches." That made her smile.

"Theo don't be such a baby. You're gonna tour until the day you die so there will always be another one for me to pop up on."

"Now it's just you popping up? You wouldn't even do the whole thing again?"

"That's not what I meant and you know it. Look can we not

fight about this please? It's a really big opportunity for me and I just want to enjoy it," she said before finally lying back on the bed and bringing me down with her. "Just think about me filling out those bedazzled leotards and try to be happy for me, okay?"

"I am happy for you. You work hard and you deserve this."

"Thank you. And look on the bright side. When I'm on her tour you won't have to go broke buying me tickets to every show," she said playfully and thankfully she kissed me again before I had to force another smile.

She was asleep in no time after I showed her what she

would be missing out on soon, but I couldn't go so I decided to stay up and take another stab at the final song for the album. There was no way for me to have known it then, but I just kind of had a feeling that I was on my way to getting all the inspiration I needed to finish it.

4
DANCING ON GLASS

Usually when I watched Tempest get ready to go out without me one of two things would happen—she would end up being super late to leave or just cancelling the plans altogether because there was no bigger invitation than seeing her fresh from the shower and oiling up her body. It got so bad over the summer that she knew better than to spend the night on days when she taught her classes otherwise she would be the one bent over and learning a lesson on tardiness.

Things played out a little differently now though after the conversation we'd had before falling asleep. Instead of pouncing on her how I usually did, I stayed in bed and tried to remind my dick that we were mad at her while she got dressed to go grab breakfast with DeeDee. He wasn't really trying to hear me out though so I had to tuck him in the waistband of my boxers to shut him up.

"You sure you don't want me to bring you anything back?" she asked for the second time since she had probably noticed me not trying to convince her to come back to bed.

"I'll get something later. All of that Casamigos from last night got me feeling real Casamiserable right now," I quipped, but the smile that it brought to her face was short-lived after I finally blurted out what I'd been wanting to say since we'd woken up. "Temp, what's the real reason you didn't tell me about this Bianca King shit?"

I knew I didn't really have much room to trip since I had only just admitted to the EJ shit, but the fact that she was capable of lying to my face for weeks still didn't sit right with me. If for no other reason than letting me know we would need to find her replacement, I should have been told the minute she decided to go through with everything.

"I already said it's because I didn't want to jinx it," she answered swearing that it was the truth, but obviously it wasn't the whole truth so I pressed the issue.

"Okay so maybe I didn't want to rub it in that Bianca had personally asked for me since I know you've been waiting to hear from her about the tour. Because it might mean that she had seen me in your show but wasn't interested in you."

I had come to the same conclusion while I watched her sleep before, but I still felt some type of way hearing the words out loud. I tried to play it cool but nothing that popped in my head was the right thing to say so the silence between us became awkward after a heavy sigh from me.

"If it makes a difference I really did try to put in a good word for you while I had her ear. I told her it would be legendary for me if she picked you because then I could maybe open and close the show."

"Wait you did what?" I asked as I threw the covers off of me since they had apparently made me mishear her only the confused look she gave said that she'd meant it. "Temp, I don't need you to get me tour placements. That's J's job so let him do it."

"Okay, but did you have to say it like that?"

"How else could I have said it? You overstepped. Big time."

Her eyes widened in surprise before quickly narrowing in a way that said they were ready to wage war on me. But instead she just nodded in agreement then icily let me know that it would **never** happen again.

We would be leaving for San Diego right after the show that night so she went back to putting everything she had used in her suitcase while purposefully avoiding eye contact with me. I'd stared a hole in the side of her head the whole time though just trying to make her look in my direction again.

Six months in and we'd literally never had a fight before because we were always good at nipping everything in the bud. Not quite ready to end our streak yet, I decided to follow the winning formula when I saw her snatch her purse up then head towards the door.

"Look my bad, alright? I know you were just trying to help and I appreciate that. I guess I'm just tripping because…Fuck it. Temp, I really don't want you to go."

She looked back in time for me to see her eyes roll. but it was softened by a lip biting grin at me begging her not to leave.

"We can talk when I get back. DeeDee is already waiting for me in the lobby."

"No, that's not what I meant. I mean I don't want you to do the Abu Dhabi shit. I want you to stay with me."

"What do you mean you don't want me to do it? How could

I not do it when this is my in with Bianca and she specifically asked for me?"

"I specifically asked for you first," I said unintentionally sounding like a spoiled kid, "and you made a commitment to this tour first."

"Yeah and my commitment ends in exactly four shows, not the added dates in January."

"Okay so what about your commitment to me then? That doesn't mean shit to you?" I challenged as she kissed her teeth.

"Theo, this ain't got nothing to do with us personally. And even if it did…like I know it's been a wild six months, but it's still *only* been six months. That's too fast to be making life changing decisions because of you and you're acting like I'm not already sacrificing enough just to be here now."

"What am I making you sacrifice to be here?" I spat before I realized how dismissive it sounded, but she returned the energy before I could dial it back.

"Oh so I'm not missing the three weekly dance classes that pay my fucking bills by being here for you?"

"Alright now be fucking for real with that shit, Temp. You ain't paid a bill out of pocket since you met me."

"Okay and? You knew bad bitches brought bills when you signed up for me," she said trying to lighten the mood, but it just fell flat and made me roll my eyes.

"Look if you were really asking me to choose between you and Bianca or you and anybody it would be you no questions asked. But that's not what you're asking. You want me to choose between you and *me* and in that case it's always gonna be me. If that's gonna be a problem then maybe we need a break while I'm gone."

"A break? Wait it's that serious to you?" I asked in disbelief as I took a step back to make sure I was talking to the same person I had just asked to start looking for places with the day before. It was still her alright, but this one had an attitude on her that I had never seen before.

"I should be asking you that. You're the one acting hella weird over nothing. I've been waiting for you to have your moment since before I even met you, but you got the audacity to actually be in my life now and pissing on mine," she said trying to shift the blame to me when she had been the one to set all of this shit into motion in the first place.

"Because look at how you fucking told me! Drunk and on accident. All you had to do was tell me back in New York and you know I would've thrown a one-man parade for your ass. But you didn't do that. You lied and now this is where we're at."

"This is not about me lying, Theo. It's about me leaving and doing what's best for me. Because if I told you right now you had to choose between me and the next leg of your tour you would not pick me so don't expect shit from me that you wouldn't even do yourself."

"But what if I did choose you? What would you say then?"

"Nothing because I would never ask you to do no shit like that for me," she spat reaching for the doorknob and attempting to end the conversation on a technicality, but I wasn't done yet.

"Okay wait. Let me make sure I got this right before you go. So you can justify letting me nut in you on the first date and that's not too fast, but now that you wanna make decisions that affect me *without me* we gotta go at a snail's pace?" I asked with just enough contempt to really make the sarcasm hit.

Off rip I knew I had committed a cardinal sin, but it was confirmed when she turned to face me again with her eyes turned down. With the time it took for a quick lick of her lips, she forced them up to focus on mine and finally found her words.

"You know…it took a minute for me to convince myself that that wasn't the dumbest shit I've ever done because of where we are now. But it was stupid then and it's even more stupid now because you turned out to be the type of little boy to throw it back in my face on Mad Day."

"Man get out of here with that shit, Temp. Ain't nobody throwing shit in your face. You just want to pick and choose the speed when it's convenient for you and I'm not letting it happen like that."

"You're not letting what happen?" she asked through an insincere chuckle. "Because as of right now we're at a dead fucking stop until I decide if I even want to bother with you anymore."

"No we're not. I told you out the gate I don't do pieces and I'm not about to be in another situation breaking up all the time. All or nothing. We're either together or we're not."

"So you're saying if I go then we're not together anymore?" she seemed to be asking for clarification purposes, but I wasn't in the mood to clear shit up when she had been the one to bring up a break in the first place

so I just shrugged my shoulders.
    "You got it then, choirboy. I guess we're not."

5
DANCING ON MY OWN

Earlier that morning I may have exaggerated feeling hungover from the previous night's bottles and bullshit, but after what might have been a breakup with Tempest I really did have a headache that I needed to sleep off. It proved to be just as stubborn as she was though because it was still there when I woke up hours later to go give away concert tickets at a local radio station.

In between all of the obligatory smiles and hugs I sulked and checked my phone to see if she had come to her senses and apologized yet though I had a feeling she was somewhere doing the same thing. I'd even tried mentally retracing our steps again because I still didn't know how shit had escalated that damn fast.

On the way into the venue for soundcheck I let Jonathan go ahead of me and I lagged behind to talk to DeeDee. She was calling from the hotel to let me know she'd finished packing to get me checked out and that she would be on her way to the arena soon. Knowing that she had been with Tempest all day I immediately tried to give her my side of the story since no doubt she'd already gotten the biased woman spin on everything.

"It's none of my business, none of my business," she playfully sang to bring my version of events to a stop. "I've learned my lesson and I'm staying out of your relationship mess this time."

"If that's the case then how do you even know something's wrong, *Deidra*?" I asked sarcastically before reminding her that the literal meaning of her name was *she who chatters.*

"Well *Theodore*, I just spent the last hour helping Tempest clear out her bunk on the bus so an educated guess told me something was amiss."

Shit. Even though they were both small and she still had to share them with me, I knew how much she loved the privacy we got from everybody else with my room and bathroom. Willingly leaving them meant she was either really serious about taking a break from me or she really wanted some attention after our argument.

Either way I knew I couldn't feed into it since it could set a dangerous precedent for our relationship going forward. That plan lasted all of two seconds though because my ears perked up at the sound of the familiar jingle that I knew only came from her wrists.

"Ay hand Temp the phone real quick," I said getting ready to just give her a little bullshit apology to get it over with before things went any further.

We only had a few more days left on the road and since she was clearly going to concert bootcamp with Bianca King after Thanksgiving next week, I didn't want to leave our status in limbo. I wanted us to be able to enjoy the last days on the road the same as we had done the firsts so I treated my pride and feelings of being right like I'd done my dick that morning. I tucked them in my waistband.

"I'm not with her anymore. I'm trying to get my sorry excuse for a suitcase closed," she grunted out before I heard a loud, triumphant zip.

"Why are you lying? I know she's right there. I just heard her bracelets when she walked by."

"Oh right," she said right before I heard them banging around again. "I'm supposed to give these back to you, but can I keep them? Because giving her jewelry to the next bitch would be bad juju for you, but giving it to your hardworking and loyal baby sister, that's just what good brothers are made of."

Oh okay. So that's what we were doing.

I had only confirmed it the day before, but I knew all along that she'd known what those bracelets represented. And not even bothering to return them to me directly said way more than any of the mean, petty words we'd exchanged earlier.

She had really been on one with that move, but I kept my head level as I finally went inside the arena because I knew how to be on one too.

Soundcheck went good as usual so I sent the band and everybody else off to do their own thing until showtime. All tour long we had been scheduling the checks earlier than they needed to be since after Tempest liked to do a quick run through to maybe add or take out something that didn't fit with the different size or shape of the stage.

But for some strange, unknown reason I just didn't feel the need for more rehearsal then so when I saw her and the other dancers coming out I went to exit stage left. I had just enough time to get a nice little nap in and since now I apparently had the whole bed to myself I was about to roll all over that motherfucker.

"Theo, where you going?" Jonathan shouted up at me since he had been watching down from the audience during soundcheck. Word had already gotten back to him about Tempest's bunk being cleared out so of course he'd checked in to make sure there wouldn't be any issues between us.

"They got it. I know what I'm supposed to do," I said intentionally being short before heading back to the bus.

By the time my intro music came blasting through the arena

speakers that night my headache had thankfully been long gone. But I wouldn't exactly credit the Tylenol I'd taken since it was more like a little hair of the dog and then a lot more hair of the dog until I realized that the theoretical Fido would probably be patchy as hell by that point. Having a drink or two before a show wasn't exactly unheard of and every now and then I would take a shot to relax my nerves, but the second those flashing lights hit my pupils I knew I was in trouble.

After the accident I'd went months without drinking and I still only had a sip every now and then so with my tolerance at an all-time low everything seemed to hit me at once. Song after song I felt the music coursing through my veins like venom and all of those old hurt feelings resurfaced then mixed with the new ones that'd been caused by Tempest.

Lyrics that had been written long before I ever knew she existed were suddenly about her and making me see her in a whole new light. And for the first time ever when I looked over at her I wasn't happy to see her.

Our temperaments couldn't have been more different though because even in my haze I could see that she was still in her zone and didn't seem to be affected by what'd happened between us. With how I was feeling I'd expected our usual fun show to be at least a little tense and awkward, but it wasn't at least on her part and that bothered me.

Antagonizing her to get a reaction actually started off pretty tame, but it quickly escalated because she managed to keep her cool and improvise whenever I did something she wasn't expecting. Like the first time I slapped her butt, she let it slide because it was technically a part of the flirtatious choreography only I wasn't actually supposed to make contact.

The next time I did it I helped myself to a handful too when she was seductively coming up from a bend in front of me. That made her miss a step, but she recovered and hit the next one then continued like nothing was wrong until I was one song away from the end of the show. Maya was coming out to my right as Tempest and the other dancers were exiting to my left when I gave her one final sendoff with a heavy-handed, open-palmed smack that would have been audible if we were somewhere quieter.

She had just knocked my

hands away as discretely as she could before when I'd touched her, but that particular love tap was hard enough to sting and forced a genuine reaction. Her reflexes had her fists balled up like *Arthur*'s in no time, but instead of rocking my shit like she obviously wanted to do she just stormed past me in a hurry to get backstage.

Jonathan had been in his seat and watching from the side like usual so I saw him jump up and follow after her, but it was all I managed to see because that was when Maya took hold of my face to bring my attention to her as she started serenading me. I tried to focus on what was in front of me instead of how I'd just let a little liquor and emotions get the best of me, but I couldn't when I heard scattered booing from the crowd during my parts of the duet.

I hadn't been heckled in years so I eventually shook it off and figured my mind was just playing tricks on me, but the mean screwface I got from DeeDee when I got backstage confirmed that they were real. Without even saying a word she just held up my phone to show me how many and how fast my Twitter notifications were coming in. During the walk back to my dressing room I read some as I chugged a Gatorade and wiped the sweat from my head.

Apparently me messing around with Tempest on stage had pissed off a few special snowflakes in the crowd and they were already talking shit and sharing clips. I sighed with relief when I realized it wasn't anything serious then muted my notifications and gave it back to her. She advised me to get Jonathan on it as soon as possible, but I explained that there was nothing to handle. Nobody who actually touched grass on the regular cared about a few petty smacks on the ass.

Shit I smacked it for sport during sex just to see it wobble and defy gravity like it did so well. And if we were keeping score I could argue that those same cheeks had slapped me up way more since she went crazy when I ate it and hit from the back. Of course I couldn't defend myself in those words to my sister though so I sanitized it some as I wished that I could put her on mute too.

"You that big of a doofus that you can't tell the difference between touching her in a private bedroom and a very public arena stage? Oh and after she dumped your doofy ass too? I'm telling Daddy!" she exclaimed right before I closed the door to my dressing room in her still ranting face.

Running around and sweating on stage for all of that time had sobered me up some but still not entirely so it took me longer than usual to get clean and ready for the bus waiting behind the arena. We were due in San Diego by morning because of back to back shows so there would be no hotel stops until Vegas in a couple days. It was bittersweet too because I'd planned on recreating the surprise first date that we'd had there, but I was pretty sure I needed to go ahead and put the whole thing on ice now. What a difference a day had made.

When I was finally dressed and on my way out I grabbed another Gatorade then popped a few sweet grapes in my mouth so that my rider food wouldn't completely go to waste. Usually my door would be open until I actually needed to get ready because people would pop in and out to grab stuff, but I had kept it shut until showtime since I'd been busy with the hairless dog.

I walked right into a fuming Jonathan who rudely pushed me back inside then slammed the door shut behind him. Before I could even begin to ask him who the fuck he thought he was getting so aggressive with he'd already answered.

"Are you out of your fucking mind? Theo, what the fuck was that?!" he yelled like I wouldn't be able to hear him from the barely three feet of space separating us. The drinks still had me thinking and moving slowly so it took a second to register that he was talking about the tweets DeeDee had just shown me.

"J, c'mon man I know you're not worried about a few dorks looking for trouble where there is none?"

"Where there is none? Nigga you're about to get canceled!" he spat angrily before showing me he'd already been contacted for a statement by a few urban and mainstream media outlets and we hadn't even left the building yet.

"You just had to go and violate the one dancer that's checking off every box that triggers the internet, didn't you? They're accusing you of colorism and fatphobia and all kinds of shit I can't even pronounce! If she was a they/them I would be giving you my walking papers the same way she did," he said half-seriously, but being reminded that she had both broken up with me and was leaving the tour for good soon was nothing to play about.

"Man whatever. I'll handle it," I said confidently as I felt around my pockets for my phone before remembering that I'd given it back to DeeDee.

"No you won't. Josie said don't tweet or say shit until we for sure get Tempest back on board."

"Wait, you called Josie about this?" I asked since my publicist had been on vacation and made it clear she would only be available for emergencies. "And what do you mean get Temp back on board? She's feeding into this shit too?"

"No, but I doubt defending

your name is high on her priority list after I just had to beg her to get on the bus instead of in an Uber to the airport."

Just the mention of Tempest potentially catching a flight instead of feelings had me misplacing the *un* in unbothered. Before I knew it my feet were moving faster than my thoughts to get me out of the building. Jonathan tried like hell to keep up, but his legs weren't as long as mine were so he just pleaded from behind not to do something stupid.

By the time I got out to the bus everybody was already inside, but it might as well had been empty since aside from the motor and Jonathan's heavy breathing behind me nobody was making a sound. I didn't have time to check individual faces to see who else besides DeeDee was disappointed in me, but a quick headcount accounted for all but Tempest. Before I had to ask and potentially reveal the amount of panic in my voice Evan nodded over to my room to let me know where she was.

Knocking on my own door for the first time was already weird enough and the standing wait to get a response made it even more awkward with an audience. After a second round of knocks DeeDee decided to chime in and state the obvious.

"She really doesn't want to talk to you right now."

"Oh for real? I couldn't tell," I said, gearing up for some major childish back and forth action when Jonathan stepped in to spare us all.

"Tempest, it's me. I'm coming in, aright?" he said after telling me to go have a seat until he called me in.

I didn't give any pushback and instead just sat back and reminisced on how I hadn't heard words like that since my days of scrapping on the playground then being sent to the principal's office. After plopping down next to DeeDee in the lounge I snatched my phone back from her then listened as she caught me up to speed on the evolving narrative since the Wi-Fi Mafia was moving fast.

They had found clips of me talking about wanting to ask Tempest out and trying to make it seem like I'd been sexually harassing her all tour long. I had wanted to believe she was making it up to scare me, but when I checked for myself I saw that things really were getting out of hand. I'd had my share of media training for potential situations like this, but having never actually gone through it personally still left me feeling unprepared.

The smart thing to do would have been to wait for Josie's professional advice, but since I didn't know how long it would take for her to get back to us all I could think to do was bring things to a halt by outing our relationship then trying to deflect as much as possible.

Stop with the false narratives

Everybody knows that Tempest is my girl

Y'all just bullied her into keeping us a secret in the first place

The first few responses to my tweets were generally in my favor or telling people to stay out of our business, but the tide changed right away when it was pointed out that her being my girl actually made what I'd done look even crazier. After that I just slid my phone back in my pocket where I decided it would stay since apparently I had only used it to add more fuel to the fire.

It continued to vibrate a few times for calls, but I ignored them when I saw that it was just my mama and dad. I knew that wouldn't be enough to dodge all of my parental figures' wrath though when Jonathan suddenly reappeared.

"Are you trying to see how

bad shit can get tonight? Because that's what it's starting to feel like. Didn't I tell you not to say shit?"

In the middle of his tirade about the tweets his phone went off letting me know that Josie was calling so I was finally invited back into *my room* on *my bus*. I instantly jumped up, eager to get this shit over with because I was tired and hungry and all I wanted to do was spend the night making up with Tempest. Our first real argument had gone further than either of us could have anticipated, but it was over with now and after sorting shit out we could get right back to doing us.

Except finding her sitting at the end of the bed and still in her performance clothes told me that things might end up a little differently than that. See she **hated** wearing heavy stage makeup and usually didn't let it stay on a second longer than it needed to so her still wearing what she hadn't cried off sent alarm bells off in my head.

I'd seen her eyes like that a couple times before, but it hit differently knowing that it was finally because of something I had done. I felt my breathing speed up and I had a strong urge to physically console her, but under the circumstances I knew it wouldn't be received right so I just sat next to her instead.

The screen wasn't on, but she kept her eyes on the phone in her lap and rhythmically tapped it with her thumb to keep calm. Obviously being on a bus it was a smaller than normal room that could only fit the basics, but it had never really felt that way before then because of all the love and good memories it proved able to hold over the last couple months. And being at odds with one another had it feeling like a closet then.

Hating the silence I tried to make small talk by asking Josie what time it was in Bali, but just like everybody else in the room she was sick of my shit and got right to the point.

"Until further notice, absolutely no social media. Nobody cares what you have to say until they hear from Tempest anyway," she said pointedly before softening her tone to introduce herself then apologize on my behalf like she already knew I hadn't done it.

She barely let Tempest return the greeting before asking if she felt comfortable doing a quick live video to straighten things out. I was about to veto the idea because that kind of thing was for more serious offenses when Jonathan let her know that it wasn't a good idea anyway since her eyes were bloodshot and it was obvious she'd been crying. Tempest still hadn't been looking at me anyway, but I saw her eyes shift further away from mine in case I looked over to confirm it for myself.

Josie stopped to think for a second before ultimately deciding for us to continue using our Twitter fingers to come across as more authentic. She came up with a quick and painless message for Tempest to send out, but I hated that idea too because it was way too close to the truth. It basically said that there was no sexual harassment going on, just a boyfriend acting out because of a stupid argument we'd had before the show.

"Just trust me, Theo. This will work. People forgive stupid boyfriends all the time. They don't forgive men who sexually harass their employees."

"Since when?" Tempest asked her before they shared a small chuckle. I liked seeing her cheeks perk up for a quick smile then and only wished that it could have lasted longer.

"Okay well maybe not the black ones."

"Since when?" Tempest repeated before bringing up a

music mogul that was coincidentally also in Bali avoiding the consequences of several sexual misconduct allegations.

They got off topic talking about his MeToo case for a couple minutes before Josie brought things back to how to carefully word the clarification tweet. I saw Tempest's demeanor change then and figured it was because she had almost forgotten that she wasn't just casually talking to a woman who wanted to help her. Just like Jonathan or anybody else who worked for me Josie would do whatever it took including fake bonding with her to protect me because it was a part of their job.

After the agreed upon words were released into the Twitterverse, Tempest immediately shut her phone back off then put it away like it was defective.

"I really need to go wash my face. Is that it?" she asked in a way that said it had less to do with the makeup and more to do with wanting to be anywhere but near any of us but especially me.

That was when Josie went into full fixer mode, knowing it was okay to drop the "girl's girl" act. After asking Tempest not to address the situation anymore and reminding her of my NDA, she demanded that all of the behind the scenes footage from my videographer be sent to her office immediately.

It was Saturday so already too late to avoid becoming a hot topic for the rest of the weekend, but she would make the best of it by giving me something couple-y and sentimental to share first thing Monday morning. That would guarantee good press all week before it naturally got buried by the holiday on Thursday and then we would be in the clear.

It seemed like a simple but effective enough plan to keep

things on the up and up with my career, but I knew I hadn't even come close to fixing everything in my relationship. That was why after letting Josie get back to her vacation I asked Jonathan to give us a minute alone.

His eyes instantly said, "Hell no!", but his words just made a suggestion for us to wait to talk until things had settled down some more in the morning. We both knew his advice went in one ear and out the other so fast that he didn't even have to bother saying it so after checking the time on his watch he gave in and threw his hands up.

"I don't even care. I'm sleepy

and I'm going to bed so y'all better have this shit figured out by morning. And no more fucking tweets. Give me your phone, both of you," he demanded with both hands out.

Tempest handed hers over with no hesitation probably since she had no desire to deal with the negativity, but I started to argue because I didn't appreciate him lowkey sonning me. Ultimately I gave him mine too though when I realized that I was just wasting time that would have been better spent apologizing to Tempest who was thankfully still seated and willing to hear me out.

Jonathan closed the door to

give us some privacy after leaving, but all I wanted was to get up and lock it so that we could get to our regular after show ritual. I was finally just as mad at myself as I had been at Tempest all day because if I had just kept my hands to myself I could've been enjoying a late night greasy dinner topped off with the sweetest dessert I'd ever had.

"I know you're probably sick of hearing me apologize today," I began before pulling my hoodie over my head and starting a fresh pile of clothes on the floor in front of the mirror, "but I really am sorry about all of this. About what I said earlier and definitely for touching you like that. I was just mad and drinking, but that's still no excuse and I swear on my life it'll never happen again, okay?"

I could tell that my words didn't do much to move her because literally no parts of her moved after I said them. Still I stayed patient and let her have the floor for as long as she needed it. Finally after a sigh straight from her soul she turned to look at me. The first thing I noticed was that her tears were all gone and replaced with a look that said she wanted to get her licks back. Nervous, I didn't know what to do with my hands all of a sudden so I dropped them to my side and prepared for the worst.

"What do you expect me to say, that I accept your apology? Because I don't. And I really didn't need all this drama tonight because you wanted to act like a little ass boy, throwing tantrums in public because you couldn't get your way."

"Ay Temp, I'm trying real hard to do the right thing here, but you're gonna have to stop with this 'little boy' shit," I spat letting my ego talk for me even though the real me was begging me to take Kendrick's always timely advice to sit down and be humble.

I had always been more of a

Cole fan though so I decided to let the sparks fly and go on a power trip instead. "'Cause if anybody knows I'm a grown ass man then it's you since I fuck you like I'm a grown ass man every night."

"Right because fucking somebody means you're a man. You're such a man but until an hour ago you were scared to even claim me because it would fuck with your career yet you expected me to play around with mine for you? You're right. You ain't a little boy. You're a fucking joke."

"Oh so that's what all of this is really about then, huh? You're leaving because you finally got tired of being a secret and you wanted everybody to know we were together? Congrats then 'cause they all know now even though again you lied and claimed you didn't want that!" I retorted since apparently the gloves were off now.

"Of course I wanted it!" she barked at me finally raising the volume to the level of the tension in the air. "Only I wanted you to want it too, but I knew you wanted this singing shit more so I played my role. And I'm not even mad at it because after all the dark places that dancing has brought me out of, I'm never putting anybody above it either. I thought you of all people would know that about me."

And I did. More than anybody I knew that when life got overwhelming for her she shut up and she danced. She had used it to fall in love with herself again after losing herself in a bad relationship and vowed to never let another man control her life again. Except that wasn't what I was trying to do.

"That's not the same and you know it. What did I tell you before? I said closed mouths don't get fed, right? You were the one running around here pretending like shit was cool when obviously it wasn't. How was I supposed to know that? I was good."

"I bet you were considering you're the only one benefitting from this entire situation. You got me working nonstop and wearing more hats than Ne-Yo for one fucking salary on top of getting your dick polished whenever you want. If I was a different type of bitch I would call the Department of Labor on your ass," she said snarkily and if I wasn't so pissed I would have laughed.

"Yo now I know you're out of your fucking mind. How are you not benefitting when you get anything you want from me?! You got a Money Mitch *Paid In Full*, baby mama Benz out of me and we ain't even got no fucking baby yet!" I reminded her even though I hated having to even bring up material shit, but it was the easiest way that I showed my love.

On top of everything else he had done I knew EJ had taken back the car he'd bought her which was how she didn't have one when we met. So even though that wasn't my style anyway for that reason alone I would never pull no stunts like that with her.

Plus I would never forget how happy she looked when I surprised her with it outside of her dance class. Her response proved she wasn't thinking back on it as fondly as I was though.

"Fuck you and *your* car because you can come get that bitch and anything else you ever bought me as soon as I get home. You won't ever be talking about what you did for me because I can do for myself."

"Man whatever. I ain't coming to get shit," I said as I waved off her ranting because now she just wanted to hear herself talk. "You're too old to be that prideful. Didn't you hear it comes right before the fall?"

"Fall? Baby, I'm a dancer. If you ever catch me on the floor, trust that it's on purpose," she bragged and I couldn't help but laugh at her popping her shit and being cocky even in an argument. She seemed to take it as disrespect though. "Yeah keep laughing. I see I still haven't learned how to pick 'em yet."

"Wait hold up. What the fuck is that supposed to mean?"

"You heard me. You're acting just like **him**."

"Nah I know we're both heated right now, but don't ever fucking compare me to that clown. That's taking it somewhere else," I warned her, but it didn't stop her from standing her ground.

It made me angry that she would compare wanting her to stay with me with the fucked up shit he had done and I knew this had to be the gaslighting shit that women were always complaining about. Because how in the fuck else could anybody come to that conclusion?

"If the red nose and big ass shoes fit then lace them bitches up."

"Nah if anybody is a clown here it's you. You went from a simple argument to breaking up. We couldn't even disagree and try to communicate and figure shit out without you jumping to extremes. Y'all are always talking about wanting niggas to communicate, but look where it got me."

"Okay let's communicate now then. You said you would never hurt me and I knew that was impossible because nobody is perfect. I even left room for the type of mistakes that I knew would come, but not shit like this. I don't know why you wanted to hurt me, but I know you did that shit on purpose. And one thing I've learned the hard way is to always get the fuck away once a man starts trying to hurt you on purpose."

I was left speechless because I couldn't believe that she was really standing ten toes down on the comparison between me and her ex. Yes what I'd done was disrespectful in its own right, but it still wasn't on the same level as the things she'd been through in the past with him.

After a minute or two of silence we both just kind of sat there wondering what to do next. I was still angry, but I didn't have any more fight in me for the night. My head was starting to hurt again, but I wasn't going anywhere near another drink for a while.

"Look maybe J was right. We're clearly not gonna agree on anything tonight so let's just go to sleep and try again in the morning. You can have my bed and I'll take the bunk," I said through a yawn as I stretched, trying to show one last good faith gesture since I knew sharing sleeping quarters was out of the question for now.

I could have kept it though because she instantly proved something I had always known to be true about her—without saying much she could say a lot.

"I'm good."

6
DANCE YOUR HEART OUT

The same way that it took two people to tango, it would take one plus another one to deal with the shady aftermath left out on the dance floor. Not having slept much didn't leave me in the clearest head space to do my half of the assignment with Tempest, but I was still more than committed to doing it when I woke up the next morning.

I didn't have my phone so I

wasn't sure of the time, but lying there until the first signs of morning peeked through the windows gave me a chance to reflect on the previous twenty-four hours and how weird it'd been sleeping without her for the first time in months. For the most part we both pretty much rolled all over the place, but I especially loved those nights when she ended up cuddled behind me in the fetal position with her knees and warm breath on my back.

On the other side of the bus wall I imagined her in the same position but not by choice since her long legs and thunder thighs would make the small bunk a tight fit. I sighed at how stubborn she'd been to not just take my bed, but finding out that she had even more pride than she had ass was at least something I could use to my benefit when we talked again.

For the sake of peace and good sleep for the rest of the tour I decided that I wouldn't argue back anymore even though I knew that I had been right. But I didn't really too much care about who was wrong or right anymore. All I wanted was to be solid with Tempest and not see her crying again.

I was so thirsty to talk to her that I sat up as soon as I heard the low knocks on my door, forgetting that she always just barged in because it was technically her room too. I disappointedly used the blanket to cover my morning wood as Jonathan came in to carelessly toss my phone, a direct contrast to how he then carefully placed his new iPad in my hands next.

"I need you to sign something for me."

"What is it?" I asked through a yawn as I wiped sleep from my eyes to scan it since I knew better than to sign anything even coming from Jonathan without having my lawyers look it over first. This was only a one page document though and the heading and first couple sentences got the point across.

I glanced up at him then back down at the device to make sure my lying eyes were telling me the truth and they were. It really was a non-disclosure agreement from Tempest.

In a nutshell it said that after whatever damage control Josie and Jonathan cooked up for the remainder of the tour, I, Theodore Smith would never again publicly talk about anything pertaining to her, Tempest Randall as a person, entity or brand. Signing and agreeing to no more physical or verbal contact were her new conditions to doing the last three performances.

I instantly kissed my teeth because this girl was just too damned petty. The sun had barely been up long enough to stretch and take a piss and there she was already trying to get her lick back. I knew it was serious too when Jonathan handed over the accessory pencil that he was always misplacing, but I refused it because I knew that it was all a test. Signing would be like agreeing that we were officially over and then there would be no coming back from that. I would have to test her gangsta by calling her bluff.

"I'm not signing that so you

can tell her she's free to go," I said as nonchalantly as I could before giving everything back then going in my bathroom.

"What do you mean you're not signing it? If you don't sign it she leaves. If she leaves, questions that we don't want to answer start getting asked so just sign it," he ordered to my back as I shrugged off his concern and relieved myself without saying another word.

"Theo, it's three more shows and you're both adults. You can get through this. She agreed that she won't be blocking or unfollowing or doing weird shit for attention like Nat. It's just over, alright? Everybody goes their separate ways and nobody gets hurt."

That was easy for him to say. At most he would be losing a potential tour connect for the other artists he managed, but I would be losing everything. It was nowhere near the same. After the next three shows he would go home to his wife and it would be like none of this had ever happened. But everything I'd worked to build over the last six months was crumbling because of one bad day and I was expected to just be cool with it.

Nah.

When Jonathan realized that

he wouldn't be able to get through to me this time, he walked out but not without leaving the iPad on my bed and telling me his lock code. I didn't even bother trying to remember it as I washed my hands then headed back to bed because I had no intention of changing my mind.

Not trying to get attention my ass.

My covers suddenly vibrating reminded me that Jonathan had come bearing other gifts in the form of my returned phone. Blocking out everything he'd just said and completely ignoring Tempest's second attempt at a breakup, I sent her a text letting her know to come wake me up when she was ready to talk then I went back to sleep.

When I got up for the second time I saw that the bus was mostly empty and I had missed texts from DeeDee asking what I wanted for breakfast and then another more recent one for lunch. I didn't have much of an appetite so I ignored it then went on searching for any signs of communication from Tempest, but it was the same as before— nothing.

Still full of hope, I tried to keep busy by finally checking all of my missed calls and other notifications from the night before. I saw that my dad had called…a lot. I was a little shook because I had a feeling what he would say about the entire situation with Tempest so for now I pushed the idea of returning his calls to the back of my mind.

I'd worked my way backwards through my unread text messages so the last one I got to was the first person that'd checked in on me after everything had hit the fan last night. It was just a simple, two word question from Maya.

You good?

I answered a few different ways, but ultimately I didn't send any of them because seeing her name on my screen planted the seed to a different strategy. No matter what I had done I hadn't been able to get ahold of Tempest's attention all day long so I figured that now it was about time that I try to catch hers.

So no…I wasn't good, but I was damned sure about to be.

I'd stayed in my room all afternoon, hearing people coming and going from all the different buses parked in the arena's designated lot for their acts. Soundcheck wasn't too far off so the crew had started the load-in to set up the venue for the show.

I wasn't proud of it, but I

would admit that I'd had on my clown shoes when I was coming up with a plan to get Tempest back talking to me. I even debated with myself for a while on whether or not I would actually lace them up, but literally hearing her in the kitchen pressing the button to ignore my calls had me singing the loop de loop song to make sure I didn't trip on them.

Maya answered the Facetime call on the second ring and I could see from her background that she was out at a restaurant and not on her bus. She'd stepped away from whoever she was with to talk to me and I wasted no time asking her to come kick it on my bus because we hadn't really hung out since we'd made the song. Not that we had ever hung out before that either, but that wasn't the point.

"Not you trying to use me to make your girl jealous."

"What you mean?" I asked laughing at her immediately clocking my intentions.

Apparently all the coke she'd done hadn't completely taken away her common sense so I reminded her that she'd been wanting to see the inside of my bus and that there was no time like the present since we were almost out of shows.

"I mean I've made it twenty-four years without getting my ass beat and I'll be damned if it won't be twenty five next week," she joked insinuating that Tempest would step to her.

That wasn't what I had in mind though and Tempest didn't really seem like that type anyway. But if everything went as planned then she would be stepping to *me* so we could get back talking and finally work shit out.

"Oh so I won't see you for your birthday then? That's even more reason to come through so you can tell me what you want me to get you," I offered flirtatiously and she just responded with a look. "Nah for real My, I swear that situation is dead. We both said some shit that you can't really come back from," I said sounding pretty convincing, but in the back of my mind praying that Tempest wasn't really feeling that way.

"Mm mn you still got them puppy dog eyes talking about her so just chill and that fupa will be back on your forehead before you know it," she cracked and I felt myself getting visibly defensive.

"Alright now, put some respect on her name," I said reflexively because it still bothered me whenever anybody tried to come for her weight, acting like they had never seen a bigger girl pull niggas before.

My dad had given me some advice on how to handle it though since apparently my mama had gone through the same when she got with him back in the day. And to think he was just a decent looking dude with a job so I knew it must have been a thousand times worse for Tempest than it had been for her.

"Chill. You know I like my bitches thick and double-stuffed too," she joked finally making me chuckle because she'd made her sound like an Oreo, but it would explain why I always liked to lick the cream first before eating the rest of her cookie.

"Y'all are at Duff's Doggz, right?" I asked then waited for confirmation as I improvised on the plan since Tempest had Compton's own Murda Maya just as shook as my dad had me.

Getting her to agree to bring me a couple of the restaurant's famous chili dogs hadn't been easy and after an hour had gone by I was beginning to think that she would stand me up until I heard the not so distant laughter of a few women coming through my open window.

The last time I'd checked everybody but Evan was on board since he helped the crew out with load-ins to flirt with the only woman on their bus. They had just been sitting around playing cards as usual and counting down to soundcheck with some tunes on in the background. Tempest looked in better spirits then and it sounded like she was winning a lot, but when I heard the knocks on the bus doors I sat back and waited for all hell to break loose.

"Oh hell nah! They're playing Uno in this bitch. Theo got the baby bus for real!" I heard a woman whose voice I wasn't familiar with say before a couple more started laughing with her.

"What do you need Maya?" an obviously annoyed Jonathan asked since she was apparently running late to her soundcheck.

"I'm on my way in, just Door Dashing for the superstar first. It might be a lil' cold, but I don't play about my tips," she said playfully as she held up the bag. "He's in the back?" she asked attempting to walk towards my room, but I heard Jonathan physically run interference by rising up from his seat in the lounge.

"No no no. Not today. I got it. Gone get out of here," he said trying to escort her and her friends off the bus when they had barely stepped on it.

"J, what are you doing?" I asked still from my bed since he

was ruining the plan. I literally only needed a few minutes of closed door conversation with her to set it off then she could be on her way. "Ay come here My. It's cool."

"Nah ain't shit about this cool and we not doing this today, Theo! This is how cases get caught!" he shouted at me and for a second I wondered if I was actually capable of driving him insane.

Lord knows he had definitely been putting in work and earning his percentage since the accident, but he seemed to be completely coming undone after the night before.

"What are you talking about? She was just bringing me some food since I missed breakfast and lunch. Relax."

"Nigga you don't even like chili dogs!" he said through gritted teeth and I had to put a hand over my mouth to keep from laughing at him knowing me so well that I couldn't get away with shit.

I just threw my hands up in defeat then plopped back on my bed, but a second after Maya and company had deboarded DeeDee was standing in my doorway looking displeased and ready to call me out.

"Did you really think that

was about to go down in here?"

"Ay what happened to you staying out of my business? It was only valid for twenty-four hours?" I asked sarcastically before telling her to get back to her card game.

Times like this reminded me of the drawbacks to having a close family member as my assistant because it came at a price since she felt like her opinions about my life mattered more than they actually did.

"Yeah because somebody gotta tell you when you're turning into a dirty, slimy ass nigga fucking with slimy ass hoes like that!" she spat kicking off round ten thousand and twelve of us arguing like kids.

I sprang up from the bed like Michael Myers ready to finish what we'd started last night when a calm voice, sounding out of place amongst the chaos, called out for her from behind us.

"What?!" she snapped before turning and realizing who was summoning her.

"Draw Four," Tempest said evenly as if everything we had wasn't breaking into pieces all around us. Her eyes caught mine for a second over DeeDee's head before she turned her attention back to the last card in her hand. "Uno out."

Now I might have only figuratively been up to my neck in hot water then, but I knew I couldn't be the only one who had felt the sudden chill in the air and it had nothing to do with being closest to the AC. I took it as my cue to just dead the bickering with DeeDee since she did have a point and the whole plan had disastrously blown up in my face anyway.

With nothing else to do but mope until soundcheck, I grabbed my guitar and headphones to get back to work on the song, but they were only halfway doing their job drowning out the cringy feeling I had from that whole interaction. Still stuck on the same part, I played it over and over until I got an almost frantic call from Evan.

"Ay bruh I think Tempest is leaving the tour," he said being a day late and a dollar short with the gossip he'd probably just gotten from it circulating throughout the crew.

Amused, I thanked him for keeping his eyes and ears open for me but let him know it was old news now and that Jonathan had already started looking for a replacement for the next leg.

"I'm not talking about the next leg. I'm talking about right now. Come outside!"

I instantly jumped up to look outside for myself, but the view from my window was blocked because somebody was getting luggage out from underneath the bus. Without even thinking about it I hopped into my crocs, put them in sport mode then hightailed it out of my room.

The bus was empty and it was a good thing it was since I would have knocked over anybody in my path with how fast I was moving when I saw that the luggage on the curb really did belong to Tempest. And just like when she danced she had drawn a crowd only now she was still as they surrounded her to say their goodbyes. Even Evan, who had just walked up, joined DeeDee as a traitor and disgrace to the family name.

Before both of my feet could hit the ground I heard Jonathan pleading with Tempest to do the right thing and get on the bus like we were in the middle of a Spike Lee Joint. He swore that he would talk to me again and make me listen this time. She definitely saw me coming out because she sighed then looked away as she embraced Jonathan, thanking him for taking a chance on her and trusting her vision with the shows.

On my walk over to them I

passed the bus driver who looked like he had more than enough reasons to be sick of everybody as he closed the storage compartment, but I was about to give him one more because he was about to have to open it right back up.

"You're not going anywhere. You signed a contract and we still have three shows left," I said conveniently skipping over the fact that I hadn't met her terms to stay anyway when I didn't sign hers.

"She's aware," Jonathan said sarcastically like he'd already tried to use that to get through to her.

She didn't even acknowledge my presence as she said the last of her goodbyes then checked to make sure she had her phone.

"I think that's everything," she finally said to DeeDee before they hugged one last time.

"Okay. Call me as soon as you land and then when you get home," DeeDee said and I thought it was funny considering how much she had hated her at one point and now she was apparently her sister's keeper. I couldn't have made this shit up if I'd tried to.

When a black car with an Uber decal pulled up alongside the bus I saw Tempest going for the handle on her biggest piece of luggage so I thought on my feet and grabbed it before she could.

"Temp, you know I'm not letting you leave so just get back on the bus," I said trying to sound reasonable and nonargumentative because even though she seemed like she was fully in control of her emotions obviously they had just been shaken up enough to do this.

Instead of doing like I'd said she looked past me at Jonathan like she was waiting for him to talk some sense into me. I stepped directly in her line of vision though so she couldn't ignore me, but even forcing eye contact for a few seconds didn't make her respond any differently. For a full minute everybody just stood around waiting for one of us to give in to the other, but I knew for a fact it wouldn't be me.

Finally Tempest cleared her throat then opened her mouth to speak. She looked right at me, but her words were meant for DeeDee as she grabbed her other things then kindly asked her to please send anything she might have *accidentally* left behind.

The inflection in her tone finally upset me enough to stop trying to play nice with her because this shit was beyond that now. She couldn't be reasoned with because her hurt feelings were still fresh and raw and the only thing she could do to get the upper hand back was to leave. I understood that, but at the same time letting her leave might give her too much time to wallow in the hurt…and if she did that things would never be the same again.

Going back to the failed plan with Maya, I knew I at least needed to get her yelling at me so I started saying whatever came to mind to rile her up. Because like any other man I knew that the cursing and the hollering was actually a good thing. It meant there was still a chance. But completely refusing to engage? Silence? You might as well gon' head and head out when a woman has nothing left to say to you because it's over.

"You think this shit is a game, don't you? You think I won't drag you to court for breaking a contract? Try me then," I dared her as I took a couple steps to close the space between us.

It wasn't until I was right in front of her that Jonathan jumped in between us. I didn't push him too hard but enough to get him out of my space and to let him know that I was offended.

"Move J. You know I'm not

ever putting my hands on a woman."

"I know. I know," he said attempting to placate me as he walked up on me again to get her bag. "Just don't make this any harder than it needs to be. Let her go for now."

I sighed because even though my brain knew he was right, my heart was saying fuck that. We wanted to talk to her now…before it was too late. Shit was finally getting real when the Uber driver popped the trunk, making me forfeit the last piece of pride I'd been holding onto. I'd been wearing the big shoes all day, but it was finally time for me to complete the look with the red nose.

"Alright! Okay! My bad! I'm sorry! You know I was just trying to get your attention, Temp, but don't leave! Please!" I shamelessly begged her right before Evan came over to help Jonathan hold me back so I couldn't physically stop her.

I knew he was trying to keep me from embarrassing myself over some girl since he still didn't know her that well, but he was too young to get what was going on here. Tempest wasn't just some girl and the whole situation had gotten out of control. I would be the first to admit that I'd gotten beside myself and acted out of character the past couple days, but if she was willing to come back and talk then everything would be okay.

"Yo what the fuck? Y'all are really just gonna stand here and let her leave by herself?!" I asked trying to flip it on them to get them on my side.

"Are we supposed to force her to stay 'cause I'm pretty sure that's kidnapping?" DeeDee cracked like she was happy karma had spun the block so fast on me. "And unlike you *I* can still track her location."

Her smug tone was the last straw and before I knew it I had

found myself starring in a scene out of *Desperate Times Call For Desperate Measures: The Love Edition*.

"Tempest, c'mon please don't do this! You know I need you. You know I can't do this shit without you. And most of all you know how much I fucking love you!" I yelled after her and for a split second I thought my declaration had gotten through because it made her stop in her tracks.

It was only for a second though because she picked up her feelings and kept on trucking as the driver closed the door behind her. And try as I might to get over to her, it was impossible with

Jonathan and Evan using all their strength to pin me to the bus until she had pulled off.

For a while I was inconsolable and wanted to throw hands with both of them, but they managed to calm me down and knock some sense into my head when the arena's security came to see what all the yelling was about. Jonathan diffused the situation with a couple half-truths and lies then got everybody except for the still loading crew back on their respective buses.

I hadn't even realized that so many people had come outside to see me make a fool of myself, but since it was looking like it'd be the only good show I would put on that night I welcomed it.

I was so pissed at everything and everybody that I almost slammed the door to my room right off the hinges and I swore I didn't have shit else to say to any of them. Realistically I knew there was nothing they could've done to stop her either, but they could have at least tried or not gotten in the way of letting me do it.

One call after another I tried to reach her but got no answer. I wanted to text but couldn't think of what to say. It didn't matter anyway because by that point my hands were shaking so much that

I couldn't hold the phone.

I tried with everything inside of me to do a better job holding in the tears that'd been building, but they did what they wanted and eventually lapped under my chin too. Thinking back on the last time I'd full on cried like that took me back to the unnerving amount of pain I'd been in at the beginning of the year.

I really didn't like having to admit that my reckless behavior had been the cause of this accident too. But I had been fortunate enough to get a second chance at life after surviving it and now I just needed to find a way to get a second chance with

Tempest.

Yes I had fucked up, but this wasn't who I was. And if it was then it wasn't who I was going to be.

Some people might've felt like I was too young and jaded to feel this way, but I was tired of standing up in love and I didn't want to spend the rest of my life in and out of it. I wanted to fall then lie down in it for good. But all I could do for now was lie down in the hard bed I'd made because I hadn't been listening hard enough back when she told me that she couldn't take another heartbreak.

I had ran off the bus to stop

her in such a hurry that I'd forgotten to turn off the music so it was still playing when I went to put my headphones up. Checking the time, I saw that I unfortunately still had plenty of time to blow before soundcheck so I picked up right where I'd left off as lyrics that could only come from living them started falling out of the sky for me like waterless raindrops.

They say patience is a virtue
Damn I needed some
Swear I never meant to hurt you
But you're still bleeding love

7

I WANNA DANCE WITH SOMEBODY WHO LOVES ME

The last date of the TheoSoul tour was another sold out show at the Staples Center so it got me home the day before Thanksgiving. Growing up it had always been one of my favorite holidays, but I found myself not really looking forward to it now that it was here. Not even my favorites, the baked macaroni and cheese, cornbread dressing and country ham could get me excited since eating myself into a food coma would be put on hold this year.

Like the snitch that she'd always been DeeDee followed through with making sure my dad got all the details to what had gone down between me and Tempest the other night so of course I'd been dodging his calls for days. I knew it would only make things worse, but I needed to keep my head in the game and off of him and Tempest to finish off the last couple shows.

When I called to tell everybody that I'd made it home

safely that morning he actually sounded pretty level-headed for once, but I learned that had just been because my mama was still in the room. As soon as she left he let me know not to get too full tomorrow because he had dusted off the old boxing gloves from the garage and planned on going a few rounds with me for showing my ass in public and disrespecting Tempest.

It had been years since I'd done something dumb enough to have to tussle with him, but I gulped and accepted the consequences with no further word because it was justified. Looking at him you wouldn't be able to tell since he was rounder now and had sold insurance all his life, but you couldn't tell my dad he wasn't Joe Frazier when he put those damned gloves on.

Tempest'd had a saint's worth of restraint to spare me that night, but it looked like I would still have to take a couple body shots as punishment since I was a trash technical boxer and my footwork was laughable. I could already hear what he would say as he landed each blow too.

Bink.

You want somebody to treat your sister like that?

Bink. Bink.

You want a man to treat your

daughter like that?

Bink. Bink. Bink.

I made a mental note to wear a few extra layers, but after wincing at the yet to happen hits I thought about Tempest's dad and how he might be feeling about everything. I had only met him a few times and despite being a retired cop with a gun collection that would make the NRA blush, he'd never tried to pull the overprotective dad thing with me. He just told me to be good to his baby girl because she had been through enough and I gave him my word that I would.

I'd been wrong when I thought that I had just failed

Tempest with my actions because when I really thought about it I saw how I had failed both of our families and even myself. I was just thankful that she had listened to Jonathan and didn't do the childish blocking and unfollowing shit that most people did during breakups. She still wasn't answering any calls or responding to my texts though so logically there was only one thing left to do.

Well technically there were two things, but leaving her alone still wasn't an option yet. She had stopped sharing her location with me, but it was Wednesday so I already knew where she would be that night and checking her Instagram stories confirmed it. Luck was on my side because it wasn't too far from the Staples Center so I was able to slip out of soundcheck then go straight to Seventy-Seven Studios without anybody even noticing I was gone.

A quick chat with the receptionist had her letting me in the studio early since there wasn't a class before or after Tempest's on Wednesdays. Still I hadn't been expecting to sit there alone with my thoughts for so long. I had forgotten to charge my phone after getting in that morning so it was already close to dying when

Jonathan began calling back to back right before seven.

A frantic all caps text let me know that the opening act was getting ready to go on soon, but I turned my phone off anyway. I needed to conserve the battery for as long as possible because I knew I couldn't leave without fixing this first. Even with a little traffic I was no more than twenty minutes away, but with as much as I had to apologize for it might take a while.

Surrounded by a room of ceiling to floor mirrors I was forced to literally and figuratively take a hard look at myself and ask what I was doing and why I was doing it. The obvious answer was that I did still have a lot of maturing to do to successfully be with a woman like Tempest. Because knowing how to make her come and buying her whatever she wanted just wasn't enough to go the distance and I knew now more than ever that I wanted to go the distance with her.

Especially after seeing the video that Josie had made from all of the behind the scenes footage the other morning. Ordinarily I would have been against something so obviously PR, but watching all of those moments had me tearing up again by the end. Some of it was shit I didn't even realize was being filmed or pictures I didn't remember taking.

I'd never paid attention to just how much I smiled when she was around and the last couple days had just intensified those feelings. I lost count of the amount of sneaky smiles, stolen kisses and sweet touches we had given each other. Making sure she was standing at my right for the prayer before each show. Our *Mr. & Mrs. Smith* Halloween costumes. It made me realize that not sharing your love with the world didn't necessarily mean it was fake, but even under these circumstances proudly putting it out there now just felt good.

And I wasn't about to let myself get used to being without her when so many good things had naturally came from being in love with each other. I guess I'd thought that making room for her in my world would mean something to her, forgetting that she didn't need mine because she already had her own. And her missing the Vegas show the previous night had hit me hard, but it also taught me another lesson worth learning—she had been right when she said that the show could go on without her just fine, but I knew *I* couldn't.

I had to get my baby back.

About half an hour had passed when I finally heard the doors to the studio opening. All the contemplating I'd done had me slouching in my seat some so I straightened out my spine and hoped that she was in a good enough mood to receive everything I had to say.

It was obviously a kids' class day because instead of heels and high cut shorts she was dressed in comfortable sweats and sneakers. I watched while she sat her bag down as her free hand instinctively went to turn on the overhead lights. When she realized they were already on her eyes scanned the room until they landed on mine.

She froze in genuine surprise or what I hoped was genuine surprise and not out of fear. Because after learning her story I knew that she was all too familiar with how bad things could get for a woman following a breakup. I sighed hard because I hadn't been thinking about any of what she had already been through when I was acting out.

"Cat still got your tongue?" I asked playfully trying to let her know that I had come in peace, but she just tucked her lip between her teeth then leaned against the door with crossed arms.

"Okay that's cool because I kinda just wanted you to listen anyway. I know this has been a really fucked up week for us, Temp, and I'm sorry. I take full responsibility for everything. But in a weird way I'm glad it happened because it made me realize that I'm not just with you because we fit and it's easy. Because even now that it's getting hard there still hasn't been a second where I wanted to walk away. I know I got a lot more growing up to do and if you give me one more chance I promise I'mma do it in record speed for the both of us."

I let out a relieved breath when I finished talking because I had said a mouthful and because it actually seemed like she had thoughtfully taken my words in from her change in demeanor. She didn't look particularly upset or even tense anymore, but her suddenly breaking eye contact to check the time pretty much said all that needed to be said. She was only humoring me because we were in her professional setting now, but the minute her class started she would want me out of her studio and life again.

"This is probably a bad time to tell you this, but I think class might technically be cancelled today since I bought all the spots. But if you really feel like dancing, I hear there's a sold out show not too far from here that could use you."

Her arms dropped from their crossed position as she charged towards me, instantly forgetting all of that restraint she'd shown just the other night.

"Why would you do that? This shit is not a joke, Theo! This is my fucking job!" she shouted as she jabbed her finger into my chest.

"And the tour ain't my fucking job? But look where I'm at instead? About to get sued for missing a show for you."

"So go then. I'm not keeping you here."

"No. Being here is more important." I put my hand on top of hers but made sure not to return it just yet. "You were right. I'm a hypocrite too because I chose my career over you. You know how bad I wanted to follow you to the airport the other night, but I didn't because I had a show to get to. I put me first and I'm sorry for not letting you do it too."

"But why do you even have to frame it like that? Like yes it would be cool when our professional paths crossed, but we don't got to have static when they don't align for whatever reason.”

"You're right. I just don't want to fight anymore." I got too overzealous and reached for her other hand which made her take them both away then take a step back.

"Fighting ain't the issue here, choirboy. It's how you fight. Abuse isn't just physical and just like I don't want to be hit, you can't toy with my emotions when you don't get your way either. Your problem is that you're spoiled by everybody around you. Your team does it. Your mama does it. You pay DeeDee to do it and now you expect me to do it too. You're never held accountable for anything!" she said getting herself worked up again so I tried to calm things down before we lost the little progress we'd made with at least getting her to talk to me.

"I know. And it's no excuse. It's just that…Temp, when I think about what we got and how fast we got here…I never thought I would meet somebody like you let alone have to share you too," I admitted as she let me step inside her comfort zone again. "I wasn't playing when I told Maya that I was stingy with you, but I'll do better. Having to share you with the world is the hardest thing I'll ever learn to do, but I promise that as long as you always come back home to me I'll let you go wherever you want to go."

She was trying hard not to fold, but I could see from the way she was still nibbling on her bottom lip what she was thinking about. Getting herself worked up at me had heightened all of her emotions and now that I was saying all the right things her entire body was reacting to me but especially below the waist.

I took advantage of it by pressing her back up against the door as my front pressed into hers. Even tied down to keep them from bouncing, I could feel her nipples trying to harden up underneath me.

"C'mon Temp, you know you've been missing me just like I've been missing you. And you know I can't go too long without my melodies from heaven," I said mannishly with my mouth close to hers as I ran a hand down to flick her clit through her joggers.

"I thought I told you to stop saying that," she laughed out as she moved my hand then balled her face back up. She was still trying her best to stay mad, but it was too late because I had practically seen the electricity jolt through her from that one touch. "Do not pass go. Do not collect $200. Go straight to hell."

That made me grin and I decided I might actually risk it all by playing Monopoly with her and everybody else one of these days.

"But why though? You think God don't already know how you be down here making it rain on me?"

"Theodore Smith!"

"*Rain down on me,*" I sang in her face just to really mess with her and keep her cheeks swollen with laughter. "So are we good now?"

"No, but I might let you keep begging at my feet later on if I feel like it. Right now you got a show to get to," she said trying to separate our bodies, but I wasn't budging an inch.

"They can wait," I said while trying to tease her by sucking on her lips how she liked before I decided to stop relying on our sexual chemistry to fix us. Because even as explosive as it was, we had been bigger than that from the very beginning.

"Temp, I'm scared if I leave now you might change your mind again. And I've been thinking about our future a lot these last couple days. We still got too much cool shit to do to let this be the end."

"Like what?" she asked letting her curiosity get the best

of her.

"Like have a big dance off at our wedding reception. Everybody knows you're gonna win, but I'mma still give it my all so don't count me out, a'ight?" I asked and I swear my soul smiled when she slowly nodded in agreeance.

"And you know I still want to make you come on every continent…except Antarctica because I'm really starting to believe that ice wall shit you keep sending me on TikTok."

That made her smile so I put my hands around her waist then pulled her in close again to say the most important reason why I would never be ready to break up.

"And don't forget we still got a gang of lil' Birkin babies to make," I said trying to keep it light because I knew how rightfully sensitive she was about her issues with fertility, but it still tensed her up and made her sigh.

"You can stop now. I've heard this type of apology too many times to count."

"Not from me," I said hoping she could see the sincerity in mine as I brought her lowered eyes back up by lifting her chin.

Her already chubby cheeks puffed out some more as she let out a deep exhale, but I couldn't smile at them anymore when a couple tears broke through then cha cha slid down her face. I wiped them away then pulled her into a tight hug as she continued speaking into my chest.

"Forgiving people has gotten me hurt and in more trouble than anybody should have to go through. Please don't make me regret still being stupid enough to do it with you because I really, really don't want to regret you, Theo."

I opened my mouth to give her a few more reassuring words, but before I could get them out I felt my eyes welling up too. Hearing her talk like that wrecked me on impact and right then and there I vowed to do everything I could to never become a part of her past. And to never have the next nigga hearing the same things about me because I would make sure there was never a next.

We stood there for a while not speaking and just holding onto each other until I remembered that I'd brought her something. We had already said all there was to say, but I still wanted to drive home the point in a way that I knew she would especially love.

I turned my phone back on, praying that it didn't die on me as I pulled up the song I'd just finished the night before on the bus. It wasn't exactly the toxic anthem that the label had wanted from me, but it turned out to be exactly what I needed to say to her.

She had pretty much lived in the studio with me over the summer so I knew exactly which adlibs she loved the most and I used plenty of falsetto at the end because she always said it gave her chills. We'd already dried each other's eyes before the song started, but by the time the track faded out mine were wet again thinking about how close I had come to losing my favorite muse.

"I never thought I would have to write a song like this

about you, but I guess that's why it took so long to finish. I had to actually go through it before I could get it out," I said as I cleared my throat to get all of that extra emotion out of my voice. "I know it's rough, but I'll get you the good version as soon as I can."

"Okay, but I still want this one too, Rudolph," she joked cracking on my nose turning red from crying as she wiped it for me with her thumb.

I was able to send it to her just before my phone died and I knew for sure that we would be okay when she started to play it again on the loud studio speakers as soon as she opened the file. If I hadn't known any better I would have sworn that she'd only gotten with me to get early access to my music, but the past six months had done a good job proving she was an even bigger fan of me as a person than as a singer.

While she vibed to the song the second time around I looked around the studio and realized that we were standing in the same spot as we'd been my first time there. The class had started like any of her hundreds of others, but by the time it was over we were alone and almost fucking to the sexy song she'd taught to that night.

The only thing that got in

our way then was not locking the door so it was the first thing I went to do after making up my mind about how I wanted to spend the rest of my private class time. I really hadn't come there with the intention of sex. I just wanted to get my girl back. But now that I knew I had her, I couldn't imagine leaving without fucking around and finding out what it was like to make love to Tempest in a room full of mirrors.

"Ay you remember that first night I came to your class?" I asked, not even trying to hide where I was headed with that specific line of questioning. I tried to kiss her again, but she was literally already trying to learn the new lyrics and turned her back to me.

"Nope. Go back to your little freaky R&B Diva. I bet she's willing to do it wherever you want."

"Probably, but I don't want her. I want you. Right here. Right now."

"That's nice, but on principle it's still *fuck you* for a few more business days," she said sarcastically as she continued dodging my kisses from behind.

"Nah what I gotta do to expedite the process? You want me to get you your own bigger studio so your classes can't sell out so fast anymore?" I offered already knowing what her answer would be.

"No, I want you to leave and get your money back so I can open up this class to my kids."

"Fuck them kids," I said half-seriously until she looked back at me over her shoulder. "Okay, I'll make it up to them. Next class is on me too, a'ight? But today, this class is just for me. And I'm really curious to see how you're about to give me my money's worth," I teased her as I pressed myself into the same ample cheeks that I'd had a less than friendly run in with last week.

"But--"

"Aht aht. It's been a rough week for both of us and right now I think we need to just shut up and dance for a little while."

Even though the new track had turned out to be a "Baby Come Back" type of song, the hypnotic loop provided a perfectly sensual soundtrack to lay Tempest down on top of my hoodie. The floor was still just as hard as I was by that point, but my hungry, wagging tongue kept her preoccupied enough not to mind too much.

"You missed me, Temp? Tell me how much you missed me," I demanded right into her sweet lower set of lips.

"Mm Theoooo. I was only gone for two days," she whined out as I anchored her thick legs over my shoulders to keep her from squirming away.

"I know, but I don't even want to go two seconds without you again."

It took two and a half replays of the three minute song to make her come the hardest I'd ever witnessed. The arch in her back got so deep it almost looked like she was levitating when her butt started to lift off the floor. She was gushy wet by the time she came back down and despite the bottom half of my face being just as soaked, I kept sucking and slurping on her until she pushed my head away.

"Yeah it's time for the private studio. You can't just be out here leaking on these people's floors like this, Temp," I teasingly admonished her as I inspected how she'd already drenched my hoodie.

Two stiff fingers and more greedy licks than I could count to her center had her whimpering and splashing me again in no time. I couldn't tell if it was because I was really putting in work or because she knew I was sprung enough to actually follow through with my words. But when there was finally no more doubt to if she was satisfied or not I had mercy on her pussy and stopped making it Harlem Shake on my fingers.

I let her catch her breath some while I undressed, but I reminded her that it was a show day when I rested my head beside hers. Knowing that I had to save as much energy as possible, she gladly took the lead then sprang into action without a word.

"Shit!" I hissed as she used her love to give me a warm, wet hug and welcome me back home.

As I pushed all the way inside I willed my dick to keep his head up, stand tall and stay firm long enough to do what needed to be done to make her never want to leave me again. I wasn't sure if she had necessarily tried to, but she made it an even bigger feat by staring down as she began rocking and rolling her hips on top of me. Being overstimulated like that out the gate was a recipe for a quick finish though so without hesitation I requested some grace to go with the mercy that I'd just shown her.

"Ay watch the mirror. Not me," I said half-seriously since it was what she told me during rehearsals whenever I got distracted by her movements.

Her triumphant grin was nowhere to be found after

glancing up at herself for a split second. I saw her instantly fall in love with her own bare reflection as the hands that she'd been using to help her ride me like a bronco left my chest to feel on her own.

"Mm mn. Don't start getting extra because we're in here. Just keep dancing on this dick like you always do," I grunted out a critique of her performance like I was in a director's seat.

But as much as I would have loved to make a home movie with her one day, ultimately I knew it would never compare to experiencing how uninhibited she was and how nasty she got when she knew nobody was watching us.

She took my advice then a deep breath before closing her eyes and opening up enough to take me all the way to the hilt. It felt so good I had to raise up to actually see it for myself and if it weren't for my own eyes witnessing it going in and out I would have bet my life that I was slipping into another dimension instead of her.

"Fuck. That's my good girl," I said encouraging her to keep doubling down on her gallops even though I could see from her face that she was already getting close.

She used all the strength she

had left to thrust herself up and down so hard on me that her breasts slapped the top of her stomach. I cupped then squeezed them with my palms, noticing for the first time how perfectly they fit in my hands. After swiping her nipples with my thumbs I sucked both rubbery buds into my mouth then started getting prepared for the incoming flood.

"Open your eyes," I demanded before begging her to tell me how good it was feeling.

My pleas fell on deaf ears as she struggled to do anything but continue to ride and keep her eyes on the prize. I knew my dick was too good to be ignored, but I let it slide and kept her plugged up as her entire body began to violently pulsate around me.

"See. You see how sexy you make frowning look when you come?" I asked while haphazardly rubbing her clit since she was so damned slippery I almost fell out. "Mm you recognize yourself? Because that's the face you make when you're getting fucked right," I groaned out after unexpectedly talking myself right into a nut too.

I braced myself for the inevitable explosive conclusion then held on to her tightly as we swapped spit and just about every other body fluid including sweat and orgasm induced tears. Collapsing backwards into our pile of clothes, I felt like I had just *Naruto* ran for miles while she smiled and climbed down from me with barely a couple hairs out of place.

"Is this the reason you couldn't even go a few days without trying to spin the block?" she teased me as she put her hands back on my chest to feel how fast my heart was beating.

"Hell yeah and you ain't ever got to worry about giving my parking spot to nobody else. Might as well gone and paint my name on the curb right now," I joked while still struggling to catch my breath.

My ears perked up when I heard my song starting over again from the speakers because it had almost been drowned out underneath our moans and all the juicy music orchestrated by our bodies. It made me remember that even as much as I wanted to stay and proudly bask in her afterglow, I had somewhere else to be and I wanted her to be there too.

"So are you gonna come back and do the last show with me? You know we weren't shit without you up there," I exaggerated to butter her up because objectively they were still good shows.

But a Tempest production without Tempest just wasn't the same. They felt off brand. Vegas was especially weird considering the last time I had been there I was with her and seriously talking about getting married when we came back.

Her absence had definitely been noted by fans talking about it online too and some were arrogantly celebrating that they had successfully gotten rid of her even though it'd actually been my handiwork. They were being just as toxic as I had been lately, but I was about to go put a stop to it for good.

I promised that if she came back I wouldn't ever let anybody hurt her ever again including myself. It was the last show, but I was ready to go out with guns blazing because I had to make them follow my lead by respecting her the most, out loud and in public. Because none of my recent success would have been possible without her and we were all about to start acting like it.

She liked the idea of me addressing my fans and standing up for her, but she still didn't necessarily want to be there on stage when I did it. She assumed it was something cooked up by Jonathan and Josie to reel back in the fans I'd pissed off over the weekend, but I explained that neither of them knew anything about my plans.

"Theo, Bianca's not picking you to open her Revival tour," she blurted out to stop me from rambling and it certainly did the trick. "I talked to Ainsley this morning and she said you were at the top of the list until…" she began but didn't finish because the reason was evident.

Everybody knew about Bianca King's zero tolerance policy for nonsense and I'd surrounded myself in too much of it to be up for consideration any longer. I was disappointed because I had done it to myself, but after accepting the blame I decided to search for something sweet in the bitterness.

Yeah performing in stadiums would have been cool and the arenas I'd been in the past couple months were a dream come true, but there was no law that said I couldn't scale it down and do smaller venues in whatever city she found herself in. A more intimate tour so soon after arenas might look like a step back to most people, but getting to be with my girl while we both did what we loved couldn't be considered anything but a win in my book.

"I'm probably gonna be real heated about it later, but right now none of that stuff even matters because…" I hesitated before quickly deciding that just because I was creative and wrote songs for a living didn't mean I had to come up with some new and innovative way to say the same old thing, "because I love you and I'll follow you anywhere, Tempest. I didn't just say it because you were leaving the other night. I meant that shit and I've meant it for a minute."

I confessed that none of what'd happened the past week had been about trying to dim her light like she'd probably thought.

It was just that I'd been out here thriving on another level ever since she came in my life. I was charting, selling out shows, making some of the best music I'd ever made and now I was even dandruff free and glowing.

There had been a lot of evidence supporting the claim that my light could only shine with hers next to me and me starting to believe it was the real reason I didn't want her to go. Always my biggest cheerleader, she sat right up to make sure I heard every word she was about to say and I knew they would be meaningful when her warm lips promised that they would always tell me the truth.

"You never needed my light. Yours has been blinding people long before we met and I know because it's what drew me to you. I think we just got even brighter when we got together," she said putting a more positive but still palliative spin on it which warmed me inside because I loved being the hero in her story. And her believing in me made me feel greater than I knew I was.

The new song restarted for the umpteenth time and I was finally getting tired of it so I reached over to her phone to turn it off.

"You know I would take it all

back if I could, but since I can't at least we got another hit record out of it," I suggested trying to find another silver lining.

"No *you* got another hit out of it. All I got is a reminder to stop dating niggas who make music. My next man will be a dentist," she said acting like we weren't automatically back together after talking then rolling around like that. I played along though.

"Say you'll take me back and I'll give you some points on it."

"How many?"

"Uh I don't know. How many inches I got, Temp, seven or eight?" I asked smugly and didn't have to wait long for the cute smile that instantly spread across her lips.

"Well it's definitely over five so I think that means we have to at least round up to ten, right?" she asked playfully trying to sound unsure, but I would have agreed to whatever she wanted because I'd heard her loud and clear about feeling underappreciated for the amount of work she'd put in for my tour.

In this business even if your worth had been proven ten times over like hers people like Jonathan would still lowball you just to see if you would take it since most did. And speaking of him it was finally time to get over to the

Staples Center before he went crazy.

"It's a good thing I didn't sign that NDA because I'm about to go violate it and tell the whole world how much I love you too," I said before giving her one last nick on the lips.

"Hold up. I'm coming too," she said before sifting through the clothes on the floor to find hers. "I want to see a few of those little heffas cry when they see me because I am not going nowhere with my birthday, Christmas *and* Valentine's Day on the way."

"So you're just gonna skip over our first MLK day together? What, you think I don't have a dream too?" I asked just to get another smile out of her.

"Just to be safe I'm not making any concrete plans because who knows what you might get into between now and then?"

"Well if our first fight was about me wanting you around more I think it's safe to say we're gonna make it."

"Really? Well since you can predict the future then why are you here and not out there playing the lottery?"

"Didn't you hear the song? I already hit the lotto and you're my prize."

"Maybe you could sing that

last part for me one more time before we go?”

By that point in my life I felt like people had been making song requests for as long as I had been alive, but I had never been so happy to fulfill one as I wrapped her in my arms and watched her while she watched me back in the mirror.

With everything I had inside of me I happily sang my love right alongside the lyrics into her ear.

Won you, lost you
You're still the ultimate prize
Can't stop, won't stop
'Til I can call you my wife

FOLLOW ME

Thanks for reading! If you don't want to miss out on any updates about future works of mine then find me on all social media platforms as TanSaidWhat, sign up for my mailing list, and join my reading group Turning The Page With Tanzania Glover.

Visit www.tanzaniaglover.com

And if the cover art took your breath away as much as it did mine, check out the talented artist Aaronya Medici! Thank you so much for bringing this couple to life!

THANK YOUS

I said that I was done writing dissertations to my family and friends in this section so I'll try to keep this brief especially since my love for them has remained the same since the first time I did this. But I do want to say that I feel like the luckiest person in the world to be able to go on this journey with people who genuinely love and care for me. Because of the immense amount of love and support that I receive from them, I get to do the thing I love most in the world and I'm forever grateful for it.

TANZANIA GLOVER

www.ingramcontent.com/pod-product-compliance
Lightning Source LLC
Chambersburg PA
CBHW032244310726

48973CB00008B/2283